Death by Design
A DIY Diva Mystery

by

Paula Darnell

For information, email Cozy Cat Press, cozycatpress@aol.com or visit our website at: www.cozycatpress.com

COZY CAT
PRESS

ISBN: 978-1-946063-77-9
Printed in the United States of America

10 9 8 7 6 5 4 3 2 1

To my wonderful daughter Andrea with much love and special thanks for her help in recipe testing and great suggestions for *Death by Design*

Chapter 1

"Ladies and gentleman," I began with a smile to the lone male student in my DIY Perfect Pillows class. Bud, a stocky, balding man, was a recent retiree and widower who'd enrolled in my class so he could learn to make new cushions for his outdoor furniture. So far, he'd completed one passable pillow and had started a second. Bud returned my smile with a grin and a bow, eliciting giggles from his classmates.

The whirring of sewing machines ceased, and my students, all fellow residents of Hawkeye Haven, our guard-gated community, looked at me attentively.

"Before we wrap up today, I have a couple of announcements. You're all doing such a great job I thought some of you might be interested in entering your projects in the creative pillow contest Suzi's Fabric Shop is sponsoring. First prize is a $200 gift card at Suzi's. I'm going to pass out the brochures with all the details." I threaded my way between the sewing machines, distributing them to the students who wanted to enter the contest.

"Bud?" He shook his head as I extended a brochure.

"Don't think I'm ready for prime time yet, Laurel."

Jennifer, a cool blonde who always made me think of an Alfred Hitchcock heroine, surprised me by also declining a brochure.

"Are you sure, Jennifer? You have such a wonderful eye for design, and your craftsmanship is superb."

"Hey, teacher, you didn't say anything about *my* eye for design." Bud mugged as he winked at me, and I obliged him by turning red.

"Gotcha. You're way too gullible, Laurel."

I had to agree with him on that score. My boyfriend Wes wasn't above teasing me himself. After my sleuthing had led to a killer's confession a few months ago, Wes had dubbed me the "DIY Detective," but my handsome guy was the real deal—a homicide detective with the Center City Police Department. Ignoring Bud, I turned back to Jennifer.

"Please consider entering, Jennifer." I knew that the gift card prize probably didn't motivate her in the slightest, but I hoped recognition of her design talent might.

Hesitantly, she accepted a brochure. "Well, I suppose I'll enter if you really think I have a chance."

She quickly scanned the brochure, pulled a small notebook from her oversized Gucci handbag, and began to make some sketches.

"Just one more brief announcement, and you can be on your way, or you're welcome to stay and work on your projects." Although class would officially end in a couple of minutes, the Hawkeye Haven Community Center's exercise facility, indoor pool, and craft rooms remained open, day and night, to all residents. The open-door policy, initiated by the new homeowners' association manager was a welcome change. Only a few months earlier, locked doors had been mandated by the previous manager, who hadn't trusted instructors with keys. Sometimes, I'd had to search for a staff member to unlock a classroom door.

"It's a different type of contest. Although you could make pillows for this one, too, it's much more involved. The Center City Paint Company will give a $1000 cash prize for the best bedroom makeover. The makeover would involve painting or wallpapering a bedroom, dressing the bed, and replacing window coverings. If any of you are thinking about redecorating a bedroom, you might want to enter. Of course, you'll need before-and-after pictures. I don't have a brochure on this contest, but I wrote the link on the board that goes directly to the contest information on the store's website. Any takers?"

"Too late for me," my friend Amy, a petite brunette, said. "I redecorated my bedrooms last year."

"It's a big project," twenty-five-year-old Amber Johannson, the youngest member of the class, commented. "I can paint like a pro, but when it comes to sewing window coverings, forget it. I can barely sew a straight seam, as it is."

"Actually, Amber, I don't think you're required to make the window treatments, pillows, or bed coverings. I know a lot of you have the skills to make them yourselves, but I believe that's optional."

"In that case, I might give it a whirl," Amber replied. "Our guest room certainly needs sprucing up." She pulled out her smartphone and punched in the link. "You're right, Laurel. If the contestants don't have to do any sewing, maybe I'll just make a couple of pillows and buy everything else."

Not surprisingly, none of the others seemed interested in the paint store's contest. Who could blame them? Unless they'd already planned to redecorate, it was unlikely anyone would do it just to enter a contest.

"Uh, oh. Snow's starting up again. I think I'll go before it gets any worse," Cynthia, a take-charge woman known for her organizational skills and participation in numerous clubs and charitable organizations, said. "I'm still sore from falling on the ice last week."

Bud nodded. "Oh, the snow, the beautiful snow. Step on the snow and down you go. Damn the beautiful snow."

"Too true," Cynthia said. "Did you make up that rhyme?"

"No, it was my grandpa's saying. He was a lifelong Iowan. He lived to be ninety, so he saw plenty of snow in his day."

"It's a love-hate relationship; that's for sure," Amy said. "New snow looks so fresh and lovely, but after a few days, the piles of snow with the sand and dirt mixed in just look sad and depressing. Oh, well, nothing we can do about that."

"Only two more months of winter, ladies," Bud said. "It'll be over before you know it."

A chorus of groans followed as most of the students turned off their sewing machines and began to pack up their pillow projects.

Amidst the activity, I noticed that Jennifer had pulled out her little notebook again and was copying the Web link I'd written on the board. Although Jennifer made exquisite handcrafted projects, her sense of design really made her stand out among my students. Plenty of students had top-notch technical skills and could follow instructions or patterns to produce a project, but creativity and innovation weren't their strong suits. Jennifer's original designs wowed me, though, and I hoped she'd showcase her talent by entering both contests. I'd noticed that she hesitated to call any attention to herself, preferring to remain in the background, although her beauty and spot-on fashion sense made her noticeable, despite her retiring ways.

The students drifted out of the classroom until Amber, Amy, Cynthia, and Jennifer—all members of my book club as well as students—were the only ones left.

"Don't forget that tomorrow's book club meets at three o'clock, instead of our usual two," Cynthia said. "You're all coming, right?"

We nodded. I didn't admit I'd failed to read the British mystery we'd be discussing. I figured I'd have time to skim it before the meeting, though.

"I just loved the book's quaint tea-shop setting," Amy exclaimed.

"Girls, in keeping with the book's theme, I'm planning to serve afternoon tea. We'll do it up right with little cucumber sandwiches, scones, clotted cream, butter, jam, and some sweet tarts—the works," Cynthia said. "Pete even volunteered to polish my silver tea set. I confess I haven't used it in years."

"What a wonderful idea!" Amber said "I'm really looking forward to it."

"Cynthia, you're always on top of things," Jennifer said, "and I agree. It's a great idea."

"I'll come over early to lend you a hand," Amy, who lived across the street from Cynthia, said. "I'm glad our meeting's at your house tomorrow. I hate driving in the snow."

"Speaking of which, just glance outside now. It's starting to look like a white-out," Cynthia observed. "Say, isn't that Bud cleaning off your car, Amber?"

"Sure is." Amber tapped on the window, but Bud, several yards away, intent on his task of clearing snow from the front windshield of Amber's car, didn't hear her. "He must be cleaning off all our cars. There he goes to yours, Amy."

"That's nice of him," Amy said, pulling on her coat. "We should go before he has to clean them all off a second time."

The others murmured their assent. "Coming, Laurel?"

"You go on. I have to duck into the office for a few minutes to check next month's class rosters. I'll see you tomorrow."

We walked together down the hall, and I waved as

they left before I continued on my way to the administrative offices. The receptionist wasn't there, but the new HOA property manager spotted me from behind her glass-walled office and came out to greet me. I couldn't help thinking again about the enormous change that had taken place in Hawkeye Haven since the HOA's former president's murder a few months earlier and the discovery that both he and Patty, the former property manager, had been involved in nefarious plans to line their own pockets at the expense of Hawkeye Haven's property owners. Although it was satisfying to know I'd had a part in solving the murder, I was happy that the incident was behind us, and the residents of Hawkeye Haven could once again live in a peaceful community.

"Laurel, it's nice to see you," Colette, the new property manager, said. "What can I do for you?" No insults, no ranting and raving, no sarcasm—instead, a pleasant smile and a helpful attitude: I certainly didn't miss Patty.

"I thought I'd pick up the class rosters for next month."

Colette searched the top of the receptionist's desk and quickly located a folder that contained my rosters. "Here they are, Laurel," she said, handing them to me. "How's the DIY Perfect Pillows class going?"

"Really well. Some of the students are planning to enter the pillow design contest sponsored by Suzi's Fabric Shop."

"That's great! I hope one of our students wins."

"Actually, I think one of them has an especially good chance of doing just that."

"What fun! That would be great publicity for Hawkeye Haven and your class. Any hints who the student is?"

"I'd better keep mum on that score. I wouldn't want

anyone to think I had some kind of influence if she does win. I'm not one of the contest's judges, but you know how gossip flies around here."

"Say no more. I understand completely. We'll keep our fingers crossed, but do let me know if she wins. I'll want to put an article in the newsletter."

"Will do."

As I approached the community center's front door, I groaned, seeing that the snowfall had intensified in the few minutes I'd spent visiting the office. One of the custodians had cleaned off the walkway to the parking lot, but snow had already covered it again. As I pulled my suitcase full of class supplies behind me, snow covered the parallel tracks of the suitcase's wheels, along with my boot prints, as I made my way to my silver Honda SUV. I'd kept my head down, stepping carefully, and I didn't see Bud behind my SUV, whisking the snow away, until I heard him call.

"Laurel, you're all set."

Startled, I jumped, slipped on an icy spot, and struggled to keep my balance. "My goodness, Bud. I'm sorry. I didn't see you back there."

"Didn't mean to startle you, Laurel," he said, looking contrite. "Let me stow your suitcase in the trunk for you."

"Thanks, Bud, and thanks for cleaning off my car, too. I don't think I'll ever get used to these Iowa winters." Winters in Seattle, my hometown, tended to be mild by comparison.

"I'm a native, and I'm still not used to them. Looks like this snow storm's going to be a real lulu. See you in class next week, teach." With a wink and a wave, appearing to be in no great hurry, he ambled toward his truck, parked on the other side of the lot.

I had a feeling he was at loose ends since his retirement and his wife's death. I could certainly empathize. I'd felt lost after my husband died in a terrible accident. Although five years had passed, I still felt his loss keenly. I'd worked hard to build a new life—moving to Hawkeye Haven at my cousin Tracey's encouragement; concentrating on my career as the DIY Diva, with several books to my credit; and teaching DIY classes at the community center. And now there was a new man in my life, the only man I'd dated since Tim died. Sometimes, I felt a little guilty about that, although Tracey, who's not only my cousin, but my BFF, assured me that I shouldn't.

As I cautiously drove out of the parking lot, I set my windshield wipers on high. Even though the wipers whipped across my windshield at a frantic pace, they barely kept up with the fat snowflakes bombarding my car. I drove the short distance home at a crawl because of the poor visibility. By the time I pulled into my garage, a couple inches of snow had settled on my Honda. I hopped out, leaving the suitcase filled with my class supplies in the trunk to retrieve later. Now, I had a more pressing matter to attend to: playtime with Bear, my chocolate Labrador retriever, who'd begun to bark in excitement as soon as he'd heard me. When I opened the door to the hallway, Bear rushed me, dancing around in little circles and pausing occasionally to let me pet him.

"Did you miss mommy, Bear?" I cooed. My pet had a way of laying a guilt trip on me every time I left him home alone, but I was onto him. Curious to know how he acted after I departed, I'd installed a home security camera and had been pleased to learn that he snoozed most of the time.

Obviously well rested, Bear barreled down the hall, raced through the kitchen, and stopped just short of the patio door. Then he turned toward me, whipping his head back and forth.

"Okay, Bear. We'll go play in the snow." I slid the patio door open, and he ran outside, his big paws leaving tracks across the patio in the new-fallen snow.

Before I joined him, I quickly changed into jeans, a warm winter jacket, and snow boots. I dug my knit cap and mittens out of my pocket and put them on, too. Although only a few inches of the white stuff had accumulated on the patio, the back yard was a different story, with over a foot of snow covering the ground. Bear loved to frolic in it, forging new pathways every time he fetched his hard rubber ball. Inevitably, I tired of the game sooner than he did, and after half an hour of tossing the ball for my eager Lab, I felt like an icicle and called it quits.

"Come on, Bear. Let's go in now."

He trotted to the patio door and gave himself a mighty shake, throwing the snow that had accumulated on his thick coat in all directions. As soon as we entered the den, I grabbed a thick towel and dried him as best I could. He flopped down on his bed, awaiting the next major event in his day—dinner.

While Bear dozed, I checked my smartphone. Still no message from Wes, who'd gone to Quantico, Virginia, for a two-week seminar at the FBI. No text from Tracey, either. She was assisting a client at a trade show in Los Angeles. My friend and next-door neighbor Liz hadn't called either. She'd decided to vacation in Florida this winter. There'd been few Saturday nights since Wes and I had started seeing each other that I'd been alone, and I missed him.

With a sigh, I resigned myself to a quiet evening at home. At least, I had an upcoming festive gala to look forward to, which Wes and I planned to attend in a few weeks, and now I'd have a chance to read the mystery novel we'd discuss at our book club meeting tomorrow. I picked up the book and became so engrossed in reading it that I jumped when Bear nuzzled my hand and pushed the book aside with his nose.

Bear might not be able to talk, but he certainly had no trouble communicating. Time for din-din.

Chapter 2

"Fantastic crowd!" I exclaimed. "We should raise a ton of money for Food for Families with this party."

"I have no doubt," Wes agreed. "Say, look at this." He'd turned to the long tables where donated items for the silent auction were displayed.

He was reading details of an eight-day trip package for a riverboat cruise on the Mississippi.

"What do you think?"

"You want to bid on a cruise?"

"Would you like to go?"

"Sure. It sounds like fun. The Mark Twain experience. It says here you have to book for June," I said, reading the fine print about the vacation package. "Early summer would be a great time to go, but what if you can't get the time off?" I knew all too well from canceled dates that Wes's job as a homicide detective for the Center City Police Department could interfere with our plans.

"I'll put in for time off right away if I win the bid. That way, I'll be guaranteed the vacation time. It's only for a few days, so it shouldn't be a problem."

"Great! I'd love to go."

"I'll put in a high bid. After all, it's for charity, right?"

"Thanks, Wes. FFF always needs donations."

My friend Amy had asked me to serve on the board of Food for Families several months earlier, when one of the members had resigned. Until I joined the board, I hadn't realized how strong the community need was for nutritional assistance for families, most of whom had small children.

"Laurel! Wes!"

I turned to see who was calling me and spotted Amy, dressed in a dazzling red cocktail gown that sparkled with sequins, making her way toward us through the crowd.

"Hi, Amy. You look fabulous! What a cute evening bag!" Amy carried a small red beaded bag that I'd never seen before. "Is it part of your collection?"

Amy nodded. "My newest acquisition. I bought it on an eBay auction, and it arrived just this afternoon. Isn't it wonderful? I figure it's at least sixty years old, but it's in pristine condition."

Wes shook his head in good-natured bewilderment. Although he would never understand our fashion obsessions, he always complimented me on my appearance. I smiled, remembering the admiring look on his face when he'd picked me up for the fundraiser earlier and told me I looked gorgeous in my turquoise blue gown.

"Great turnout," he commented.

"It sure is," Amy said.

I nodded in agreement, knowing that Marcie, FFF's president, had spent months planning the gala, and it certainly looked as though she had thought of everything. In the middle of a bleak Iowa winter, the ballroom of Center City's Grand Hotel had been transformed into a magical, lush floral paradise. Marcie planned to reveal the results of the silent auction at the end of the evening, with cocktails, dinner, and dancing to music from Bob and the Boys, the most popular band in the area, leading up to the fundraiser's finale, the announcement of how much money the gala had raised.

"Let me finish my bid here, and I'll get us all some champagne," Wes said, as he scribbled his bid and deposited it in the bid box. "Or would you rather have something else to drink?"

"Champagne," I said.

"I'll have champagne, too," Amy murmured.

"Champagne all around, then. I'll be right back."

I watched as Wes made his way through the crowd. He looked quite dashing in his charcoal tuxedo, and the smattering of gray hair at his temples enhanced his debonair look.

"Laurel, did you hear that Jennifer won Suzi's pillow contest?" Amy asked.

"Yes, she called me this afternoon to tell me the news."

"She's really talented. I can't believe how intricate her beading is on her winning pillow. Such fine work— it must have taken her hours and hours to do."

"Yes," I agreed. "She's super excited, mostly because of the recognition. She's going to take our pillow class shopping for the next project at Suzi's and pay for their materials with her prize money."

"That's sweet of her. Which pillow project is next?"

"It's the lacy neck roll with satin and ribbons, the pink and cream pillow I showed on the first day of class."

"I really like that style. It's so dainty and feminine."

"Maybe too much so for our only male student. I'll definitely have to show Bud a way to make a practical neck roll, instead of a decorative one."

"Oh, look. Speak of the devil. There's Bud now." Seeing that she'd caught Bud's eye, Amy exchanged waves with him. "It still feels a little bit strange to have a man in class."

"It doesn't happen too often; that's for sure, but Bud's making progress, and he's not afraid to use the industrial sewing machine."

"Those machines are great for heavy-duty upholstery

fabric, but I must say, I'd rather work with fashion fabrics myself. To each his own. Ah, here comes Wes with our drinks."

Balancing a tray that he'd snagged from the table near the champagne fountain, Wes arrived and distributed the drinks before giving the tray to a passing server.

"I'm impressed. You didn't spill a drop," I said, smiling at him. "You looked like a pro carrying our drinks."

Wes shrugged. "Only three glasses: that's easy. It's when you have a tray loaded with heavy dishes that you have to be careful."

"Sounds like you're speaking from experience," Amy said.

"Yup. I waited tables for a couple years during college. I didn't like it much, but it helped pay the tuition."

After dating Wes for several months, I thought I knew a lot about him, but learning this tidbit reminded me that he could surprise me. I surprised him sometimes, too. When I'd joined the board of Food for Families shortly after we began dating, he wondered where I'd find the time, because, in addition to monthly board meetings, which didn't take too long, since Marcie ran a very efficient meeting, Amy and I also stuffed food bags two or three times a week. Wes hadn't objected, though, and he managed to help out occasionally, too.

"Ladies and gentlemen," Marcie called, as she removed a portable microphone from its stand. No screeching or squealing meant that, efficient as ever, she'd tested it beforehand to make sure no annoying feedback assaulted the guests. "Welcome to our Food for Families gala, and thank you all for your generous support. It's going to be a fabulous evening. After

dinner, we'll dance to music from Bob and the Boys."
Enthusiastic clapping met Marcie's mention of the
popular band. "The silent auction results will be
announced at 11 p.m., and the bids will be open until
then, so put your best bids in to help our community's
families who need nutritional support." More clapping
broke out. As soon as it subsided, Marcie went on,
"And now, please seat yourselves. You'll find your
table number on your program that you received at the
door, and, we'll be raffling off the table centerpieces
immediately after the silent auction winners are
announced. Chef Arnold of Arnold's Bistro, right here
in Center City, has prepared us a fabulous feast!" More
applause broke out as people began locating their
assigned tables.

"We're at table one, aren't we, Laurel?" Amy asked.
Marcie had insisted that the board members and their
guests sit at the two tables in the front of the ballroom.

"Yes. I'm glad we're at the same table. You and
Marcie are the only board members I really know.
Come to think of it, I don't know Marcie all that well.
She's only attended our book club a couple times, and
she's all business at the board meetings."

"She certainly went all out for this fundraiser. I can't
wait to find out how much we've raised at the end of
the evening."

"Just look at that centerpiece!" I said as we walked
to our table. "It's absolutely gorgeous." With spreading
greenery at its base, the arrangement was low enough
that we could see across the table and easily talk to each
other. At a few other parties, I'd seen centerpieces that
effectively blocked conversation, so I appreciated this
one, not only for its lack of height but also for its lovely
yellow and lavender tulips. Although we had several
more weeks of winter to endure, the centerpiece
reminded us that spring would come eventually.

"I wouldn't mind winning that one. It would make the perfect spring decoration for my dining room table," Amy said.

I paused for a moment to admire the floral creation before Wes pulled my chair out for me. So far, we were the only occupants of the table, but in a moment, Jennifer and her husband Matt, who was also an FFF board member, came along, followed by Marcie and her assistant Josh.

After compliments all around on our evening gowns, servers, dressed all in black, appeared and began pouring wine, offering us a choice of red or white.

"Don sends his regrets," Marcie said. "He and Gladys both came down with the flu yesterday, so they won't be able to come." We all responded with sympathetic murmurs, and I was glad I'd taken the precaution of getting a flu shot in the fall. "That leaves us with some empty seats, so we invited Justin and his girlfriend to join us." Justin was Matt and Jennifer's twenty-year-old son who attended Iowa State University in Ames.

Matt scowled and turned to Jennifer. "You didn't say anything about that."

Her hands trembling slightly, Jennifer blushed. "I didn't think you'd mind."

"Well, I *do* mind. I mind very much. You know how I feel about my son dating a stripper."

Wes and I exchanged glances while Amy stared at her plate, and Marcie and Josh busied themselves sipping their wine.

"Fine," Jennifer said, although we could all tell that it was anything but fine with her. "I'll text them and tell them to sit at their assigned table." Jennifer pulled her smartphone from her evening bag, and for a split second, I thought Matt would relent, but he didn't stop her.

"I'm sorry, Matt. I didn't realize . . ." Marcie apologized. Just when I was wondering whether the situation could get any more awkward, Matt waved away her regrets and changed the subject.

"Let's forget about it," Matt said, as he launched into speculation about how much money the gala would raise for FFF. Although the tension at our table dissipated somewhat, I could tell that Jennifer was still upset by Matt's outburst. As dinner service began and normal conversation around the table resumed, I waited for several minutes until Jennifer finally joined in before congratulating her on winning the pillow contest sponsored by Suzi's.

Amy chimed in, too. "Your winning pillow is so artistic!"

I described the pillow to the group. "It's a fabulous pillow design—a peacock embroidered on cobalt blue silk with metallic threads and tiny iridescent beads. As always, Jennifer's workmanship is topnotch."

Jennifer modestly accepted congratulations from everyone—everyone except her own husband, that is.

"A pillow?" he said. He obviously knew nothing about the contest or Jennifer's winning entry. "One of your little sewing projects, I guess, huh?"

"Yes," Jennifer said, her voice quavering.

"Excuse me," Marcie said, as she slipped out of her seat. "It looks like the band's ready. I need to introduce them." Thankful for the interruption, I turned to Wes.

He leaned close to me and whispered, "Let's dance." I nodded, and as soon as the band began playing, we headed for the dance floor. Luckily for us, the band started with a romantic tune, perfect for a slow dance. Neither Wes nor I could claim to be good dancers, but we managed not to embarrass ourselves and avoided stepping on each other's toes, for the most part.

As Wes held me close, I began to relax, and I

realized that the tension level at our table had affected me. Although the dance floor was crowded, we could have a conversation without anyone overhearing us.

"That guy's a real jerk," Wes commented. "I would have said something to him ordinarily, but, since you're both on the board, and I didn't want to make things uncomfortable for you."

"I had no idea he treated Jennifer like that. Even though I've been to their house several times for book club meetings, he never showed himself or else he may not have been home, so I've only encountered him at board meetings, and they're strictly business. Sometimes, Amy and I go out to lunch afterwards, and Marcie recently joined our book club, but, as far as I know, the other board members don't socialize with each other. Poor Jennifer! I wonder whether he's always like that."

"Bullies don't change. When I first joined the force, I saw plenty of ugly incidents firsthand when we got domestic disturbance calls. It was more usual than unusual to get several calls to the same address."

"Do you think Matt's beating Jennifer?"

"My best guess—probably not. He keeps her under his thumb by his words and his behavior."

"How awful. No wonder she's always so quiet, even when she's not around him."

When the band paused between numbers, we held hands and drifted back to the table where Josh was pulling out Amy's chair for her.

"Thanks for the dance, Amy. You're right up there with the pros on *Dancing with the Stars*. It's a good thing you offered to lead, or I never would have made it," Josh joked.

"No problem, Josh," Amy said breezily. "We can wait this one out and try again later, if you like."

"No, thanks, Amy. I can't keep up with you, but

maybe Matt or Wes . . ."

"Saved by the bell, Josh," Amy said. "Here comes my next dance partner now. He asked me to save him a dance." Amy stood and waved at Bud, who whisked her away after a quick greeting to us. We watched as they whirled around the dance floor to a much faster beat than the first number.

"Who would have guessed?" I said. "Bud's a fantastic dancer, just like Amy. He's so light on his feet." I noticed Marcie watching the couple as she made her way back to our table. She continued staring at them as she sat down and lifted her wine glass.

"Who's that guy Amy's dancing with?" she asked me. After I explained that he lived in Hawkeye Haven and that he, Amy, and Jennifer were all classmates in my Perfect Pillows class, she nodded. "You really can't judge a book by its cover, can you? I'd guess he's at least twenty years older than Amy and outweighs her by a hundred pounds. Amy certainly found the right partner because I don't see anyone else out there who even comes close."

"Matt, how about you and Jennifer?" Josh said, nodding towards the dance floor.

"Matt's a wonderful dancer, but . . . " Jennifer began.

"I'm having knee surgery Friday," he interrupted. "My orthopedist claims I'll be good as new after he replaces both knees. I played football in college and injured them both then, but the real kicker happened when my snowmobile overturned a few weeks ago."

"That's too bad, Matt," Marcie said, not noticing his attempt at humor. "We'll miss you at our next board meeting. Will you have to stay in the hospital long?"

"Nope. I'm planning to recuperate at home. I can't stand hospitals."

"We've contacted an agency and lined up some private duty nurses to help out," Jennifer said.

"Yeah, I wouldn't want to interrupt your social schedule."

"I can cancel the book club meeting."

"We can hold it at my house," I volunteered. Frankly, I wondered why Jennifer hadn't already suggested canceling the meeting or moving it to another member's home.

"No need. I'll probably be so out of it I won't know the difference."

Strange that he changed his tune when I said something. I had the feeling that, had Jennifer suggested the very same switch of plans, he would have objected. As the evening went along, Amy and Bud stayed on the dance floor while Wes and I danced every slow dance. During the times we were at the table, Matt was perfectly polite to me, Marcie, and Wes while he disagreed with the few comments Jennifer offered and ignored Josh. It was a relief when Marcie finally rose to emcee the silent auction. As she revealed the winners of each auction, items that included jewelry, artwork, gym memberships, spa days, and dinner-for-two deals, the buzz in the ballroom increased, and the winners claimed their prizes. To build suspense, Marcie saved the most valuable items for last—the Mississippi River cruise and a brand-new compact car. She paused as Josh presented her an envelope with the results.

"Now for our last two auction winners. First, a wonderful eight-day steamboat cruise on the Mississippi River. And the winner is . . . Wes Wesson!"

I squealed.

"All aboard, matey," Wes whispered as he hugged me.

In the hubbub at our table, we didn't even hear who'd won the car.

"Now we'll have a lottery winner at each table to take home your beautiful centerpiece. We've made it easy, folks. I'd like each of you to reach under your seat and take the card that's taped there. If there are any empty seats at your table, anyone else at the table is welcome to check them, too."

Amy rushed back to the table with Bud in tow just as Marcie was making her announcement. We followed instructions, pulling small cards out from under our seats.

"Hmmm," Amy said. "Mine's blank. How about everyone else?"

"Looks like they're all blank," Bud said after looking at his card and those he'd pulled from under the two chairs that had sat empty all evening.

"There must be a method in this madness," Amy declared.

"And the winners are all those holding a green card!"

"That's you, Bud," Amy nudged him. He'd been looking at Amy, rather than his card.

"Oh, right. Now whatever would I do with a huge floral arrangement like that? It's all yours, Amy. I'd be happy to carry it to your car for you."

"Thanks, Bud. That's really sweet of you. I love it! It's so cheerful, and it'll remind me that spring's on the way—sometime."

"'Sometime' is right," he said. "I heard on the weather report that another snowstorm's on the way. It's due to hit tomorrow. These blasted Iowa winters—they just go on and on."

I smiled because complaining about the weather seemed to be a habit among native Iowans. I wasn't any too thrilled myself to hear that another snowstorm was on the way.

Marcie wound up her speech with thanks to all the donors and attendees who had made the gala a success. We learned that we'd raised over $100,000 for FFF.

With all the planning that had gone into the event, I figured the organization would do well, but I was astounded to find out just *how* well. After congratulations all around, we said our goodbyes and headed for the door. It was slow going as we stopped to chat along the way and thank people for their support. The crowd had thinned a bit when we saw a young couple entering the ballroom as everyone else was leaving.

"Uh, oh," I said.

"What is it, Laurel?"

"See that young couple weaving their way in?" Wes nodded. "That's Justin and his girlfriend Bunny. It looks as though they've been celebrating someplace else. I hope Jennifer and Matt have already left."

"No such luck. They're still back by our table."

"Maybe we should head them off," I said.

"Too late. Matt's spotted them."

I've never seen a man cover so much ground so fast limping, but Matt reached the pair quickly.

"Just turn around and get out now," Matt said loud enough for us to hear. "You're drunk, both of you."

"We only had a few drings on the way here. Say, where's everybuddy going innyway?"

"The party's over, you fool. Now take your little stripper and leave."

"She's not a stripper. She's my fiancée!" His defense of his girlfriend might have been a little more dignified if he hadn't hiccuped when he said "fiancée."

"Over my dead body," Matt yelled. "If you marry her, you'll never see a dime of my money. I'll cut you out of my will!"

"Go ahead. See if I care. We're in looove." Punctuating that declaration with another hiccup, Justin grabbed Bunny by the arm, and they lurched back toward the entrance.

"Laurel, I have to say, FFF certainly throws a memorable party," Wes said.

"And how," I agreed.

Chapter 3

"Look who's here, Bear." I opened my front door, and my BFF Tracey stepped inside, but she'd barely cleared the door frame when Bear ran to her and bounced around, blocking her path. After she reached down to scratch him behind his ears, just the way he likes, he poked his nose into the open tote bag she was carrying.

"That's right, Bear. I brought you some treats," she said, making a circular motion with her free hand. "Let's go into the kitchen."

Bear bounded ahead of us as we walked into the kitchen, and Tracey pulled out a container of treats she'd made for Bear and set it on the counter.

"You had him at 'treats,' but 'kitchen' sealed the deal," I told her. Bear wagged his tail as Tracey opened the container and produced a couple of dog treats. While Bear crunched them, I hid the container in the pantry. Although Bear didn't normally counter surf, I'd caught him with his big paws on the edge of the kitchen counter only a few days earlier. His guilty look when I saw him told me he knew better.

"Looks like we got the same memo this morning," Tracey said, making a sweeping motion with her right arm. "Tunics, skinny jeans, and boots, right down to our long, dangly pendant necklaces."

"Great minds and all, right?" The main difference between our ensembles was that while Tracey wore fashion boots with four-inch stiletto heels, I'd opted for a more practical low-heeled version with a rubber sole.

"I guess we should get going," Tracey said.

"Okay." I grabbed my coat and handbag and slipped on some warm knit mittens that Amy had given me for Christmas. She'd knitted a matching scarf, too, which I slung around my neck. We were on our way to our monthly book club meeting, and I wanted to fill Tracey in on what had happened at the gala.

"Stay home and be a good boy," I admonished Bear as we left the house. He looked at me with sad eyes, and I knew he'd be waiting at the door for my return.

Tracey hadn't attended last week's fundraiser because she'd been out of town on a business trip, so I dished as she drove us to Jennifer's.

"I was amazed that Jennifer insisted on having the book club at her house when we could have easily switched it to mine, but that's what she said when I talked to her yesterday. She called to tell me that she won the Center City Paint Company's bedroom makeover contest."

"She won that, *too*?" I'd texted Tracey about Jennifer's pillow contest win. "Wow, she must be a terrific designer."

"Jennifer's very talented, but she certainly doesn't broadcast it. At first, she wasn't even going to enter either contest, but I encouraged her, and she decided to do it. Anyway, she told me that Matt came home in an ambulance yesterday morning, and it would be easier to keep an eye on him if she held the meeting at home."

"I guess that makes some sense, but our meeting might disturb him. We're not always quiet."

"That's true. Sometimes everybody talks at once, but Jennifer said Matt's on some heavy-duty pain meds, and the doctors told her he would probably need those for the next few days. I guess he'll be so out of it that he won't know the difference."

"Well, let's hope so because it looks like the gang's

all here," Tracey said, motioning to four cars parked on the street. Since residents weren't normally allowed to park on the street (HOA Regulation 52 states that "residents must park in their garages at all times unless visiting another resident"), we figured the cars belonged to our club members. Tracey pulled up in front of a neighbor's house, and we hurried across the street, dodging a big pile of snow beside Jennifer's driveway.

Jennifer greeted us at the door and hung our coats in her hall closet, and then we joined the group in the living room.

"Do you know if anyone else is coming today?" I asked Jennifer.

"Just the seven of us." Besides Jennifer, Tracey, and me, Amy, Marcie, Amber, and Cynthia were all there. Tracey and I sat on a love seat, facing the sofa where Amy, Cynthia, and Amber had settled, while Jennifer and Marcie both sat in chairs that Jennifer had placed strategically to make an intimate rectangular seating group. As usual, Jennifer sat closest to the dining room so that she could slip through it, into the kitchen, to check on the refreshments. Jennifer and Matt had a full-time cook who also did some light housekeeping, but Jennifer always liked to make sure that everything ran smoothly.

Soon we were engaged in a lively discussion of the month's book selection. By tradition, we took turns having the meetings at our homes, and the hostess of the month selected a book that she thought the group would enjoy reading. Jennifer had picked a family saga that spanned several generations. We had fun talking about the life choices some of the characters made, and the time passed quickly.

I had to admit that I looked forward to the refreshments at each meeting almost as much as I did to the book discussion because all our members, except me, were excellent cooks or bakers, so there were always some homemade goodies to savor. When it came my turn to hold the meeting, Tracey always pitched in and made the food. We joked that she'd inherited the family cooking gene, whereas, I, on the hand, sadly had not.

Jennifer had disappeared, probably to check on Matt, but Katie, her cook, was bustling about in the dining room as she arranged trays and set up a fondue pot on the large sideboard. The dining room table had been set for seven, with china, crystal, and sterling silver flatware, not to mention the embroidered yellow cloth napkins, matching table runner with silk and beaded tassels on each end, and place mats. I had no doubt that Jennifer had made the beautiful table linens herself. Although Cynthia, and sometimes Amy, went the more formal route when serving the club refreshments, the rest of us tended to be more casual, relying on disposables to make the cleanup easier.

"I think we're ready now, ladies," Jennifer said as she placed a bowl of angel food cake chunks next to the fondue pot. My mouth watered for the delicious dark chocolate fondue. Katie, Jennifer's cook, had made it a couple times before, and it had always been a big hit with the chocolate lovers in the group. "Please serve yourselves while I pour the wine." She hesitated. "Wine all around, right?"

Nobody objected, and she began pouring Chardonnay into the sparkling crystal wine glasses that were set at each place. Encouraging Cynthia to take the lead, the rest of us formed a line behind her and filed by the sideboard, helping ourselves to apple salad, artichoke quiche, and crusty homemade bread accompanied by cute butter pats molded into flower shapes. A stack of smaller dessert plates sat next to the fondue pot, awaiting our second trip to the lovely buffet.

"How's Matt getting along?" Marcie inquired.

"He's sleeping now, which is probably a good thing," Jennifer said. "We arranged for 24-hour nursing care because Matt insisted on coming home to recuperate. He's taking some very strong pain medication at the moment. Tomorrow he starts physical therapy."

"I went to the sports therapy center after I had shoulder surgery," Amber said. "I was glad it's so close, and I didn't have to drive across town to get there because my shoulder was really killing me at the time."

"I've been there, too," Cynthia volunteered. "They seem to do a good job."

"We have a therapist coming to the house, starting tomorrow," Jennifer said. "With a double knee replacement, it's going to be a while before Matt's mobile again."

"Oh, no. Both knees at the same time? I'm sorry to hear that," Amber said. "I didn't realize he'd had *both* knees replaced."

We'd just begun to eat when Justin burst into the room, followed by Bunny in a tight red sweater with a deep V neckline and the skinniest skinny jeans I'd ever seen. When she tossed her long blonde hair like a rambunctious young mare, Justin gazed adoringly at her and seemed to forget his mission for a moment, but after Bunny nudged him, he spoke to his mother.

"Mom, do you mind if we grab a plate? Don't worry; we won't disturb your group. We're playing pool, and we could use a break, but we're going back down to the rec room."

"Of course, darling. Help yourselves. I thought Katie was making you a tray, but she must have forgotten."

"I didn't forget." Katie had popped up behind the young couple. "The tray's in the kitchen, but Justin wanted more bread, and they don't have any chocolate. I told him I'd bring it later, but he wanted it now."

"It's fine, Katie."

"Everything is delicious, Katie," Tracey said, in an attempt to mollify the disgruntled cook, and we all voiced our thanks.

"You want more? I'll bring more now."

"Yes. Thanks, Katie," Jennifer said, and Katie scurried back to the kitchen. It was probably a good thing because Justin had commandeered the remaining bread and the rest of the quiche while Bunny had speared mounds of angel food cake and dipped it in the chocolate fondue.

His plate piled high, Justin grabbed Bunny's right hand with his left and pulled her toward the kitchen. "Thanks, Mom. You all have a great time," he said to the rest of us, as the couple disappeared into Katie's domain.

"My, Justin looks so handsome. I keep thinking of him as a little boy," Cynthia said. "And his, er, friend is certainly well-endowed."

We all laughed at this understatement.

"Bunny's a nice enough girl when you get to know her," Jennifer said. "I have a feeling that she had a tough childhood, but she never really talks about it. She's a student at the community college." Remembering that Matt had called her a stripper at the FFF gala, I briefly wondered what the real story was, but I soon forgot about it as the table buzzed with chit chat, and I joined in.

Just as I was contemplating whether or not to help myself to another serving of yummy chocolate fondue-covered cake, shouting, followed by a loud clattering noise, erupted from the kitchen, startling us all.

Jennifer rushed into the kitchen, and Tracey and I followed her, hoping we could help with whatever domestic crisis had happened. I stopped when I saw who was shrieking at Katie—my nemesis Edna, a student of mine and a former nurse, whom I'd briefly suspected had killed the president of our homeowners' association six months earlier. By accident, I'd discovered that Edna, who'd been a board member of our HOA at the time, had a motive for murdering its president. He had found out that she'd lost her nursing license and had been blackmailing her with the information, forcing her to support his voting position on issues that came before the board. As it turned out, Edna was innocent of that crime, but, along the way to finding out who the real murderer was, Edna had threatened me, and she'd never forgiven me for suspecting her or for knowing what I knew about her. Only Wes and Tracey knew the truth about Edna's background. I certainly hadn't shared it with our neighbors, but Edna hadn't taken a class from me since, nor had she spoken to me when we saw each other around the community. These actions didn't upset me, but I did disapprove of her dispensing medical advice when I knew that she'd barely escaped going to prison for using dirty needles on her patients, some of whom had contracted hepatitis C as a result.

"9-1-1, Katie! Call 9-1-1!" Edna yelled, but Katie just gaped at her. At her feet lay an overturned steel cookie sheet.

"I'll call," Tracey said, running to the house phone. *Thank goodness for landlines,* I thought. None of us had a smartphone within reach. "What's the matter, Edna?"

"It's Matt! There's something wrong! Tell them we need the paramedics."

"Come over here and tell them exactly what's wrong," Tracey urged, holding the phone's receiver out to Edna, but Edna didn't step forward to take it.

"Tell them he's not breathing," she said.

"Oh, no!" Jennifer ran down the hallway to the sickroom, the very same bedroom that she had redecorated for the paint store's contest.

I followed. When we rushed into the bedroom, the room that Jennifer had decorated beautifully in blue and cream with gold accents, we saw Matt lying in a hospital bed. If I had just glanced at him from the doorway, I would have thought he was sleeping.

Jennifer grabbed Matt's shoulders and shook him in a vain attempt to rouse him while I took his wrist and felt for a pulse, but there was none, and his arm felt cold. We looked at each other, and I shook my head.

"I knew he should have stayed in the hospital for a few more days, but he wouldn't listen to me, as usual," Jennifer said, as tears dripped down her face.

Tracey appeared at the doorway. "Help's on the way." We could hear sirens already. Residents of Hawkeye Haven were lucky that there was a Center City fire station within a few blocks of our community's back gate; the CCFD rescue unit was on its way.

Tracey joined us at Matt's bedside, but as soon as she saw our faces, she knew.

"It's too late," I whispered.

"Jennifer, come and sit down," Tracey guided Jennifer to a plush armchair. "I'm so sorry," Tracey murmured, as she squeezed Jennifer's hand. Jennifer looked up at Tracey.

"Could you please put that blanket over him, Tracey?" Jennifer asked. "He hates to be cold."

"Of course." Tracey took a plaid blanket from the dresser top and spread the blanket over Matt from his shoulders to his toes. "Surgery complications, probably," Tracey murmured.

"Look at his face," I whispered.

Tracey looked, and I could tell from her reaction that she'd seen what I had, but before she could say anything, the CCFD team arrived, and we moved next to Jennifer to give them room. They gathered around Matt's bed, speaking in voices so low we couldn't hear them until the team leader distinctly said, "Call the police."

"Ladies, please wait in the other room," one of the firefighters said.

"But why?" Jennifer asked. "Why can't I stay with him?"

"It's procedure, ma'am."

"Come on, Jennifer. Wouldn't you like to go upstairs and lie down?" She allowed us to lead her back down the hallway to the kitchen, but when I tried to steer her into the foyer to go upstairs to her bedroom, she stopped.

"No. No. I should be here. Justin—where's Justin?"

"I'll get him," Katie said, opening the basement door and shouting for Justin to come upstairs..

"At least come into the living room and sit down, Jennifer," Tracey urged.

Jennifer nodded. Cynthia, Amy, Marcie, and Amber gathered around murmuring their sympathies in an effort to comfort her as we settled Jennifer on the sofa.

"Mom, what's going on?" Justin asked as he came into the room. "Katie said you needed to see me right away."

I motioned for our book club group to come out into the foyer so that we could give the grieving mother and son some privacy.

"Do you think we should leave?" Amber asked. "Or maybe a couple of us should stay here to help."

"We could offer, but I'll bet they'd rather be alone for a while," Marcie said.

"We can't leave," I said.

"What?" Amy said. "Why not?"

"I'm afraid it's a suspicious death. The police have been called. I'm sure they'll want to take statements from all of us."

Shocked stares greeted this news.

"Not surgery complications?" Cynthia asked. "I just assumed Matt suffered from a blood clot. That's what happened to my friend Kay after she had surgery."

"I don't think so," I said.

"How do you know, Laurel?"

"I don't know for sure, but I probably shouldn't say anything until after we've talked to the police."

As we were talking, Edna sidled out from the kitchen and crept slowly towards us. Her short gray hair poked out from under an even grayer knit cap, and she was bundled up in a heavy winter jacket, knit scarf, and snow boots. I couldn't imagine how she thought she'd get past us without our noticing her, but that appeared to be her goal. She'd gone in back of Cynthia and was reaching for the front door handle when I stopped her.

"You'd better not leave, Edna," I cautioned.

She glared at me. "You can't stop me, Laurel McMillan."

"No, but I can," Justin yelled, his face red, as he moved swiftly toward the door. "You did it! You killed my father!"

Chapter 4

"No. No." Edna protested. "I didn't do anything wrong."

"You're the one who was supposed to be taking care of him. Some nurse."

"Please, Justin. You've got it all wrong. I wasn't even there."

"What?" he yelled even more loudly. "Where *were* you then?"

"Uh, I just stepped out for a minute. Your dad was asleep, and with all the drugs I gave him, I knew he wouldn't wake up soon."

"Is that how you did it? You gave him an overdose, you miserable excuse for a nurse." Justin lurched toward her, and I doubted that we'd be able to restrain such a strong and determined young man.

"Justin?" A quavering voice called. Evidently Bunny had just emerged from the basement recreation room and had no idea what had happened "What's wrong?"

"My father's dead, and she killed him!" he said, pointing to Edna. Although he sounded angry, Bunny's appearance calmed Justin somewhat. Bunny rushed to him, hugging him, and he sobbed in her arms as Edna furtively edged closer to the front door.

Honestly, I didn't know why Edna was so determined to leave. She lived just down the block, and, even if she went home now, the police could easily find her at home to question her. Perhaps she didn't plan to stay home, though. *Did Edna really have something to hide?* I wondered. If she hadn't been keeping an eye on

Matt, what *had* she been doing?

For the second time that afternoon, sirens wailed as the police responded to the rescue team's summons. Four uniformed officers trooped up to the door where Edna had frozen as soon as she heard the sirens, and, before we knew it, we were all cordoned off in the living room with a caution not to leave. One officer escorted Katie in from the kitchen and stationed himself in the corner where he could keep an eye on everybody and make sure we didn't leave.

"The detectives will be here soon, and they'll need to take statements from each of you," he announced. "So just wait here."

We could see into the foyer from the living room, and we watched as the medical examiner and the crime scene technicians came in. I wondered when the detectives would arrive. Would Wes be assigned the case?

The next arrivals answered that question. I'd know that ruddy complexion and frizzy blonde hair anywhere. It, along with her eternal bad attitude, belonged to Wes's former partner, Sergeant Felicia Smith. Felicia and an older, balding man, whom I recognized from the police department's Christmas party that I'd attended with Wes, came into the living room. As soon as she saw me, Felicia scowled and groaned.

"Folks, I'm Lieutenant Dennis Walker from the Center City Police Department, and we'll be taking statements from everyone. If the family members could please stay here, I'd like the rest of you to go into the den with Sergeant Smith here." He nodded toward Felicia, and we rose to follow her. "Say, don't I know you?" the lieutenant asked as we filed past him on our way to the den.

"We met at the department's Christmas party. I'm Laurel McMillan."

His memory sparked, he said, "Wes's girlfriend, right?"

I nodded.

"This shouldn't take too long, Laurel. I understand you and your friends were having some kind of a meeting here."

"Our monthly book club."

"Okay. I'll talk to you later." I sincerely hoped he meant that statement literally because the last thing I wanted to do was give my statement to Felicia. The woman hadn't liked me from the first moment we'd met, and she definitely hadn't liked Bear, either. She'd made it clear that she didn't approve of Wes's relationship with me; in fact, she'd gone so far as to tell him I wasn't the right woman for him.

In the den, Felicia ordered us to "stay put" while she called us, one at a time, into the adjoining library. Her abrasive manner hadn't changed a bit.

Bunny chewed gum and fidgeted while Katie nervously wrung her hands and sighed, and Edna looked as though she'd like to make a break for it. The rest of us waited quietly to give our statements.

Felicia chose to interview Amber first. I thought about what Amber might be able to tell her, and I figured it wouldn't be much. We'd invited Amber to join our book club five months earlier. I'd met her when she'd taken one of my classes, and both Amy and Cynthia had been impressed when Amber had volunteered to help one of our elderly neighbors, a ninety-year-old woman who could no longer see well enough to drive. Since Amber had never attended a book club meeting at Jennifer's home before today and had never met Matt, as far as I knew, I'd put her at the bottom of my suspect list if I were investigating Matt's death.

Tracey leaned toward me and whispered, "Do you

think we're all suspects?"

I nodded. "I'm afraid so. We were all here when it happened."

"Maybe somebody else could have come in. I don't think the front door was locked. Jennifer probably left it open because she was expecting us for the meeting. I really can't believe that anyone here would have wanted to harm Matt, despite what Justin said to Edna. We know all these people, Lo-lo," she said, calling me by my childhood pet name. "It just can't be one of them. It just can't."

"I guess it's possible another person could have come in while we were in the dining room, but what about Katie? You have to go through the kitchen to get to the back hallway."

"She wasn't in the kitchen all the time. Remember she was setting up the buffet in the dining room?"

"Yes, but, at the time, we were all in the living room, and we would have seen anyone who entered the foyer from the front door."

"Oh, right. That's true. I guess it couldn't have happened that way."

"Actually, it could have," I said slowly. I almost snapped my fingers as I thought about the floor plan of the house. "What if someone came in while we were in the dining room? Katie was in the kitchen, and Edna was in the sunroom. Edna admitted that she 'stepped out' of the sickroom. Who knows how long she left Matt alone?"

"But if Katie was in the kitchen . . .?"

"There's another way into the back hallway. Remember the powder room right off the foyer has a second door?"

"Which opens into the back hallway," Tracey said. "I always thought that feature was a bit odd."

"You'd have to be familiar with the house to know

about it, though."

"Or the floor plan. There are some other homes in Hawkeye Haven with exactly the same specs."

I nodded. Of the eight Hawkeye Haven model homes, all built by the same construction company several years earlier, Jennifer's two-story house was, by far, the largest available, not quite in the McMansion category, but close.

Justin, his eyes red-rimmed, came in looking for Bunny, who jumped up and ran to him as soon as she saw him. She tried to throw her arms around him, but he sidestepped her embrace and held her out in front of him as though she were a child who needed to be instructed on what to do.

"Bunny, I'm taking Mom to Aunt Rose's house. We can't stay here. The police said we could probably come back home tomorrow or the next day. They'll let us know."

"Okay. Let's go."

"No, you can't leave yet. They want to talk to everybody."

"Oh, yeah." The way she said it made me wonder whether she'd forgotten why we were all waiting in the den.

During this exchange, white-coated techs marched through the foyer on their way to the front door. I could see they carried items from the bedroom, encased in large plastic bags. It was impossible to tell what most of the stuff was, but I recognized the plaid blanket Tracey had used to cover Matt and the gorgeous blue peacock pillow that took the top honors in Suzi's pillow contest.

Because both the den and the living room opened onto the foyer, everyone in both rooms saw the evidence bags as the crime scene technicians passed by.

Unfortunately, Jennifer freaked out when she saw the procession of white coats.

"Wait! Don't take that," she said, emerging from the living room and trying to grab the plastic bag holding her prize-winning pillow.

"Sorry, ma'am. Evidence." The man didn't stop to converse with Jennifer, and he exited through the front door before she could protest again.

"Mom, let it go," Justin said, running to her.

"But why would they need my pillow?" she wailed. "I worked so hard on it and decorating the bedroom, and now it's all ruined."

She began to sob, and, for a moment, I wasn't sure whether she was crying about her prize-winning handiwork or about her husband's death in the very bedroom she'd designed and decorated. I shook off the doubt, though, knowing that Jennifer had suffered a great shock. I told myself that anyone would feel distraught under the circumstances. It was bad enough that Matt's death had been completely unexpected. It was almost unfathomable that someone had killed him, right in his own home during his wife's book club meeting.

"Come on, Mom. I'm going to get your coat, and we're going to Aunt Rose's right now."

"Bye, honey." Bunny waved flirtatiously at Justin. Cynthia shook her head and whispered "totally clueless" to Amy, who was sitting next to her.

"Hey! I heard that." Bunny glared at Cynthia, who had the grace to look embarrassed.

Before any further exchange could take place, Amber came out of the library, followed by Felicia, who indicated Cynthia should join her. At the same time, Lieutenant Walker stepped into the den and motioned for me to join him.

His laptop rested on the coffee table in front of the sofa, where he seated himself and indicated that I should sit on the loveseat opposite.

Without preamble, he said, "I want you to tell me everything you remember from the time you arrived until the time the rescue squad got here."

Quickly, I ran through the timetable as he tapped notes on his laptop. There didn't seem to be much to tell other than that the only time I'd left the group was when I'd followed Jennifer to the sickroom. I was sure that the lieutenant was trying to establish where everybody in the house had been that afternoon. Then he asked me who else had left the book club group during the afternoon.

"I'm not positive, but I think that Amy, Amber, and Marcie excused themselves for a few minutes to go to the powder room sometime before we all went into the dining room."

"All right. Thank you, Laurel. I'll need you to come down to the station tomorrow to be fingerprinted since you were in the room where Mr. Daniels died."

My stomach did flip-flops. At my stricken look, the lieutenant sought to reassure me that the fingerprinting was just a formality and that everybody known to have been in the bedroom would also be fingerprinted. So that meant Tracey would be fingerprinted, too. *At least we could go to the police station together,* I thought.

I rose to leave, but, Columbo-style, the lieutenant asked me "one more thing: "When was the last time you saw Mr. Daniels, er, before today, that is?"

"It was at the Food for Families fundraiser eight days ago, on Saturday night. Wes and I sat at the same table as Matt and Jennifer."

"So you were friends?"

"Not exactly. I'd call Jennifer a friend, although not a close one, but I knew Matt only because we're both board members of FFF. The other times I've seen him have been at board meetings. We didn't socialize."

"You didn't like him much, did you?"

"No. Not much. He wasn't very nice to Jennifer at the party. Wes can tell you all about that."

Back in the den, waiting as the others were called to give their statements, I worried that I'd said too much. Should I have admitted that I didn't like Matt? Even though Lieutenant Walker's questioning style seemed matter-of-fact compared to Wes's when Wes interviewed witnesses (I knew because I'd once been one of those witnesses), I had an uneasy feeling. I wished Wes had responded to this call, but even if he had, I doubted that he could have taken the case since his own girlfriend was involved.

Tracey pulled out her smartphone to check her messages.

"Oh, no," she said. "I really need to call this client back, but I can't do it now. I wonder how much longer they're going to keep us here. We both gave our statements already. Shouldn't we be able to go home?"

"I wish. Bear's going to go wild when I finally do get home. It's long past his usual dinner time."

"Poor Bear. He does like to stick to his schedule."

"For sure," I agreed. "He's definitely a creature of habit. Of course, he's not starving. He only thinks he is."

"Right. It won't kill him to have his dinner late." As soon as Tracey said that, she clapped her hand over mouth. "I shouldn't be saying 'kill' after what happened here today."

"It's okay. You didn't mean anything by it."

"What *do* you think happened? Justin accused Edna of giving Matt an overdose, but he must have been smothered, I think. What do you suppose made those marks on his face?"

"I'd bet the beads on the peacock pillow Jennifer made. It kind of looked like little pit marks all over his face."

"Wow. The same pillow she didn't want them to take away. Do you think she knows?"

"I'm not sure. She didn't really seem to notice the impressions of the beads on his face, even though she was looking right at him when she was trying to wake him."

"She sure got upset when she saw them taking her pillow away."

"She sure did," I agreed.

Could Jennifer have killed her own husband with her prize-winning pillow? How ironic that he'd belittled her achievement at the gala. I wondered if he'd done the same when he'd learned she had won the bedroom decorating contest, too. Or perhaps he hadn't even known that she was a two-time winner. She hadn't told me about her success in the paint store's contest until yesterday, the same day Matt was discharged from the hospital. It was certainly possible that she hadn't told him she'd won the contest. Then, too, just because Jennifer told me about it yesterday didn't mean that she hadn't known sooner. I had assumed that she'd just learned of her win when she called me because she'd seemed so excited. I wondered when Mr. Cousins, the paint store owner, had notified her that she'd won first prize.

Time dragged on, and I hoped we would be allowed to leave soon. So far, only Justin and Jennifer had been able to leave. Both detectives had finished their interviews, and they were conferring in the living room.

"I don't suppose it would do any good to ask how much longer we have to stay here," Cynthia said. "I'm feeling rather queasy."

Katie jumped up. "I'll get you some water."

The cook didn't get far, though. The uniformed officer, who was standing in the foyer, wouldn't let Katie go to the kitchen.

"But she doesn't feel good," Katie told him, pointing to Cynthia.

"Okay, ma'am. I'll check with the detectives. Here they come now." He turned toward Walker. "Sir. . . " he began, but Lieutenant Walker motioned him to follow him and Felicia into the den.

He approached Edna, who sat alone in a corner.

"Stand up, please. Edna Elkins, you're under arrest for the murder of Matt Daniels."

We looked on in shock as the lieutenant read Edna her rights, Felicia handcuffed her, and Walker instructed the uniformed officer to transport her to the police station for booking.

"No! No! I didn't do it," Edna protested. "You know me," she appealed to the group. "I would never harm a patient."

Only Tracey and 1 knew what a whopper that statement was.

"Are you waiving your rights?" Felicia asked her.

Edna shot a pleading look around the room as though we would be able to answer the question for her. "Please," she begged.

"Are you waiving your rights?" Felicia repeated.

Out of the corner of my eye, I saw Amber almost imperceptibly shaking her head. Although the movement had been subtle, Edna saw her.

"No," she said. "I want a lawyer."

Chapter 5

Tracey dropped me off at my house and went on her way. I knew she needed to return several business calls, so I didn't press her to come in. As soon as I opened the front door, Bear came bounding around the corner toward me. He'd been waiting for me in the hallway next to the door to the garage. When he saw me, he couldn't contain his excitement. He barked and ran around in circles before racing to the kitchen and standing next to his food bowl.

"Just a minute, Bear," I said, and I slipped quickly into the bedroom and dropped my handbag on the nightstand beside my bed. "Here comes mommy."

Wagging his tail, he pranced around the kitchen as I prepared his dinner. I gave him a pat as I set his bowl on its mat and stood back to watch him devour his dinner in less than a minute. Then I pulled open the sliding glass door in the den and let him out into the backyard to wander around for a while. It had been dark for hours, so I turned on the patio light and watched him as he patrolled the perimeter of the backyard before rolling around in the snow. When he came back to the door, I was waiting for him with a large, fluffy towel, and he didn't get far before I threw it over his back and vigorously rubbed him. With his typical Labrador's weather-resistant coat, snow and rain didn't bother him at all, but he seemed to enjoy the rubdown, just as he always liked being the center of attention. When I finished, as a reward for holding still, I gave him one of the treats Tracey had brought earlier. Although he begged for more, I resisted, and he gave up, flopping down on his bed in the den and closing his eyes.

As Tracey had been driving me home, I'd tried to call Wes, but my call had gone straight to voice mail. I tried again now with the same result. Since I didn't want to text him about Matt's murder, I left him a message to call me right away. He could have been called in to work. If that were the case, he might not be able to return my call for quite a while.

I felt unsettled as I thought about the afternoon's events. Could Edna really be a killer? I could think of no reason that Edna would want to harm Matt. On the other hand, I could believe that her carelessness or negligence might lead to a patient's death. Smothering Matt, if that's what had happened, had to have been a deliberate act. Although Tracey and I had our suspicions, we didn't really know the cause of Matt's death. Obviously, the detectives must have known something that I didn't because they'd arrested Edna on the spot. I certainly didn't have all the pieces of the puzzle, and although I wished Wes would tell me why the detectives had zeroed in on Edna, I thought it unlikely that he'd share any of the details with me.

I turned on the TV and watched a movie, but my mind wandered, and I didn't really pay close attention. After a couple of hours, I turned it off and decided to go to bed. Just as I picked up the remote and turned off the TV, my phone rang, and Wes's picture displayed on the screen. At last!

"Sorry I couldn't call you earlier. We've been interviewing a suspect in an old case for hours, and we're getting nowhere. The guy hasn't asked for counsel, so we're going to keep at it, but Timmons and I both needed a breather."

"You haven't talked to Lieutenant Walker then?"

"Walker? No. What's up?"

When I told Wes about Matt's untimely demise, my voice quavered. The stress of the day's events felt like a heavy weight pressing down on me. I wished Wes were with me, but I knew he had a job to finish. If my boyfriend couldn't comfort me in person, my dog could. Bear had wandered over and put his head on my lap while I talked to Wes. As I ran my hands through his soft fur, petting him, I felt grateful for my canine companion. I continued stroking his silky fur while I talked to Wes.

"Wes, when you talk to Lieutenant Walker about seeing Matt at the FFF gala, could you ask him *why* he arrested Edna? Why kill Matt when the house was full of people and she was the one in charge of his care? For that matter, why kill Matt at all? What possible motive could she have?"

"Lots of questions, sweetheart. I'll find out what I can, but I can't share anything that hasn't gone public."

"I figured you'd say that, and I do understand."

"Let's go to dinner tomorrow night. If there's anything I can tell you then, I will."

"Dinner would be nice."

"I'd better get going. Here comes Timmons. Hopefully, we can wrap up this interview soon. I'd like to get at least a couple hours of sleep tonight."

I had the same thought, but I knew I probably wouldn't sleep much because I couldn't stop thinking about Matt's murder. In bed, I kept replaying the day's events and trying to figure out why Walker had arrested Edna so quickly.

Finally, I drifted off sometime in the wee hours, only to awake before six the next morning when Bear began to whine and nudge my arm. Although I knew he wanted to go for a walk, I didn't feel like facing the cold yet. I checked the weather forecast on my smartphone, and the current temperature was ten degrees with a predicted high of thirty, which certainly sounded better to me than ten. Bear would have to wait until afternoon for his daily constitutional. Pulling on a heavy robe, I slid open the patio door and let Bear out. A frigid blast of air hit me as he ran outside, but it didn't bother Bear in the slightest. He loved cold weather.

When Bear came in, I gave him his breakfast and promised him that I would take him for a walk later. I sipped coffee as I searched the news online for any further developments about Matt's murder, but there was nothing I didn't already know. I turned on the TV to catch the early morning local news. The emphasis of the local story was the fact that Matt's death was the second homicide that had occurred in our guard-gated community within the past six months. I watched the national news headlines next, and the gated community angle had made it a national story, too. Network reporters were calling Hawkeye Haven "Murder Haven." Definitely not good. Their stories then veered into comparisons with other murders that had taken place in guard-gated communities. Most of the reporting had nothing to do with Matt's case at all. My phone blew up with calls and texts as soon as the word spread rapidly throughout Hawkeye Haven, and most of the callers had already heard the story from one of our book club members. Neither Lieutenant Walker nor Sergeant Smith had cautioned us not to talk about the murder, so I supposed it was all right to discuss it. After all, the murder six months ago of our HOA president, Victor Eberhart. by one of his neighbors was still on the residents' minds. Now one of Matt's own neighbors had been arrested and charged with his murder. No wonder everyone who lived in Hawkeye Haven felt a sense of unease. Our neighbors were people we routinely interacted with and trusted. The entire community seemed to be in a state of shock.

Colette, Hawkeye Haven's new property manager, called me to ask for advice about whether she should honor a request from one of the local TV stations for a comment about the safety of our community. Perplexed that she'd asked me for advice, rather than the HOA's board members, I understood when she told me that she'd seen me do a couple of interviews about my DIY books with Channel 4, and she thought I might know what to do. Since I didn't feel qualified to help her, I suggested that she consult the board, and if they thought a statement should be issued, perhaps Marcie could help prepare it. She always did a splendid job of spreading the word about the need for donations to Food for Families, and I knew she had a background in public relations. As a resident of Hawkeye Haven herself, I figured she wouldn't mind helping the community.

All morning, Bear kept coming over to me and then going to the front door, but I held firm. After a quick trip to the police department for fingerprinting, I returned home to find my dog still eager to go for his daily walk. By early afternoon, the temperature had risen to twenty-five, and it was a sunny day, so after bundling up in a warm jacket, long scarf, cap, boots, and gloves, I relented, and we set out for our walk. My phone rang again just as we reached the front sidewalk. I pulled it out of my pocket, intending to tap "ignore," but when I saw Wes's picture on my screen, I answered.

"Hey, beautiful!"

"Flattery will get you everywhere," I said, smiling.

"It isn't flattery. It's true. Say, would it be okay if we go to Tony's for dinner tonight, maybe around six?"

"Sure. That's fine." I knew what was coming next. At least, I knew the gist of it, if not the particulars.

"Unfortunately, I'm going to have to come back to

work, so I thought we could grab a quick bite somewhere close. This old case I'm trying to crack has taken some unusual turns, and it's going to involve more interviews and a lot more digging. A couple of people are coming in this evening after they get off work to talk to us."

"It sounds as though you're making some headway."

"I think so."

"Did you have a chance to talk to Lieutenant Walker yet?"

"Just for a few minutes. Not much to report, but I'll tell you what I can this evening. Gotta go now. I'll see you at six."

Wes would continue to be tight-lipped about Matt's case, but perhaps I could glean some tidbit of information, and I didn't mind going to Tony's. It was tucked away in a corner of a strip mall close to Hawkeye Haven. The ambiance wasn't great, but I certainly had no complaints about the dinner menu or Tony's scrumptious homemade desserts.

Wes arrived to pick me up promptly at six, and after Wes gave a tummy rub to an insistent Bear, we left for the restaurant.

"I'm sorry about having to cut our evening short," he said, taking my hand. Work interferes with too many of our dates."

"You know I understand, don't you?"

"I do, and that's one of the many reasons I love you." We paused beside his car for a long kiss. It felt so good to be in his arms that the rapidly dropping temperature didn't register until our lips parted.

"I love you, too, and . . ."

"And you're freezing, right?"

"Did my chattering teeth give it away?"

"Yup. Let's get this show on the road."

Wes's car felt wonderfully warm as we drove to

Tony's and parked right in front of the door. Tony's daughter led us to a booth in the corner where the cold air wouldn't blast us every time a customer came in, and she took our pasta orders right away. She returned in a minute with fresh bread, balsamic vinegar, and olive oil. Although I was eager to find out what Wes knew about Matt's case, I waited until he brought up the subject.

"Walker asked me about the fundraiser, Laurel, but he doesn't think what happened there has any bearing on the case. He has solid reasons for arresting Edna."

"Okay, I can understand that she seems to have been in the best position to have smothered Matt, but I can't understand why she would want to."

"Did I say Matt was smothered?"

"No, but he must have been. Tracey and I both saw the marks from the beaded pillow on his face, and so did the rescue squad. Then later we saw the crime scene techs carry the pillow out in a plastic evidence bag."

"Hmm. I can see that the DIY detective's at work again. No comment."

"Wes," I protested, but to no avail. "What about motive then?"

"All I can say is that she has one, and Walker confirmed it before he arrested her."

"You're driving me mad! That's all you can tell me? Really?"

"Afraid so," he said. "Ah, here comes our dinner now."

"Saved by the bell."

Wes nodded. "Actually, there's one more thing I can tell you," he said tantalizingly.

"One *more* thing? You haven't told me anything yet!"

"Never say I'm not a man of mystery."

"Humph!" I said with a mock pout. I knew it was

useless to keep badgering Wes, but I felt a bit frustrated because he knew the answers to my questions, but couldn't tell me.

"Good lasagna," he said with a wink. "You know I'd tell you if I could."

"I know," I said, sighing.

"Here's something I *can* tell you, though. Edna's going to be arraigned tomorrow afternoon: Department 7, Judge Hanover's courtroom, four o'clock. Anything that happens there is a matter of public record."

"I assume it's open to the public, then?"

"Yes. Hardly anyone usually shows up for these things, though. They're normally routine."

"Thanks for the heads-up, anyway. I may just have to attend."

"Somehow, I figured you'd say that."

* * *

The next afternoon when I arrived in Judge Hanover's courtroom, I was surprised to find quite a few people already seated since Wes had told me that arraignments didn't usually draw a crowd. I recognized a few reporters from the local television stations. Although the local stations had carried the story again that morning, the national media had dropped it. Matt had been a prominent businessman in Center City, and I supposed the local media would follow any developments in the case closely. On the early morning news, Channel 4 had prominently featured Colette reading a carefully worded statement about safety in Hawkeye Haven.

Although it was a finely crafted public relations piece, I doubted that residents of our community had been mollified. In fact, some of them had been quite vocal in their criticisms of Hawkeye Haven's security when I talked with them. I thought their criticism was unfair. After all, the community's security team couldn't have prevented Matt's death. I felt sorry for Luke, our security chief, not only because he was my friend Liz's grandson, but also because he'd become the target of unfair criticism.

The attorney from the prosecutor's office, a young woman with long, brown hair, wearing a trim navy suit, placed her laptop on the table in front of her and opened it. At another table sat a distinguished-looking man with white hair, wearing a charcoal-gray suit. I couldn't see his tie from my seat several rows in back of him, but I'd be willing to bet it screamed conservative. Judge Hanover, a short woman decked out in a voluminous black robe and wearing huge bright-blue-framed glasses, shuffled some papers and didn't look up when a deputy sheriff brought Edna in.

Evidently, prisoners weren't allowed to dress in street clothing for an arraignment. Edna wore a baggy orange jumpsuit that made her look even chubbier than she was, but what really caught my eye was Edna's complexion, which looked as gray as her short, bristly hair. Her head down, she shuffled toward her attorney, who stood when she entered the courtroom. He courteously pulled out the chair next to him. Just before Edna sat down, she glanced back and saw me. We locked eyes, but neither of us smiled or waved. Edna leaned over and said something to her lawyer; then they both turned as she pointed me out to him. He nodded, and they turned around to face the judge. The judge told Edna she was charged with first-degree murder and asked for her plea.

Edna stood and mumbled, "Not guilty." Her lawyer nudged her. "Your honor," she added, and the judge directed the court reporter to enter her plea.

When Edna sat back down, her lawyer stood and waited while the judge set the trial date.

"Your honor, I'd like to re-visit the issue of bail. Mrs. Elkins is a longtime resident of Center City, a homeowner in Hawkeye Haven, and a board member of the Hawkeye Haven Homeowners' Association. These are strong ties to the community."

"We oppose bail, your honor," the prosecutor said.

The judge turned to her. "Go on, Ms. Losee," she said.

"This is a serious charge, your honor. The deceased was in the care of the defendant when he was killed, and we have physical evidence that his death was no accident, but the result of a deliberate attack. This evidence ties the defendant to the murder. In addition, I'd like to point out that Mrs. Elkins has a previous felony conviction in another state in a case that also involved a patient of hers."

"Your honor, releasing my client poses no risk to the community." Edna's attorney argued. "She's innocent of these charges. It would be cruel to require a woman of her advanced age to stay in the county detention center until the trial."

Ms. Losee started to answer, but the judge held up her hand.

"Enough. Bail is denied." She tapped her wooden gavel, rose, and exited the courtroom.

A buzz rose from the spectators in the courtroom as the judge departed. Then the reporters broke for the door. I imagined that the latest hook on the murder case would be the denial of bail to a sweet-looking, elderly woman. Edna was led away, and her lawyer stuffed some papers in his briefcase and stood.

I was gathering my coat and handbag when Edna's lawyer beckoned to me from the center aisle.

"Hello, Laurel?" He looked uncomfortable. "I'm sorry. Edna was so flustered she couldn't remember your last name."

"McMillan. But Laurel's fine," I said, seeking to ease his discomfiture.

"Thank you, Laurel. I'm Nate, by the way. I'm afraid Edna's pretty upset even though I warned her that this judge probably wouldn't grant her bail. Edna asked me to give you a message. She'd like for you to visit her at the county detention center."

"Really? I wonder why. We're not exactly friends."

"I don't know. She wouldn't tell me anything except that she was afraid you wouldn't speak to her if she phoned you, so she asked me to pass along the message. She says it's important."

"Hmmm. Well, I'll have to think about it. I don't know that I want to talk to Edna, especially in jail."

"The detention center's website has all the information you need, if you decide to contact her. It's your decision, of course. I'm just the messenger."

"I'm sorry," I said. "I didn't mean to sound harsh. It's just that Edna and I haven't spoken in six months. I can't imagine why she'd want to talk to me now."

"Like I said, up to you. Good day, Laurel."

As soon as I arrived home and pacified Bear with the last of Tracey's treats, I looked up the website for the county detention center. I learned that although professional visits were freely allowed, inmates could have only two half-hour social visits a week. Visitors could register and request a time online, and they were supposed to arrive at the detention center half an hour before the scheduled visit. Visits could only happen during limited time slots and only on certain days of the week.

Why did Edna want to see me, of all people? As I moused over the "visitor registration" button on my monitor, I had to admit I was curious to find out.

Chapter 6

As I walked toward the entrance of the county detention center, it looked every bit as dull and gray as the overcast sky above. Parking lots, dotted with huge piles of dirty snow that rose like islands out of the asphalt, surrounded the two-story cement-block building on three sides. A graveled alley ran behind it.

Stepping into the lobby, I surveyed the large room. Before I could go farther, I had to pass through a metal detector, similar to those at airport security stations. Once I'd gone through and retrieved my purse, I spotted the registered-visitors sign, and I joined the short line there. Now I understood why the directions on the lockup's website had advised visitors to show up thirty minutes before their scheduled visits. The line moved at a glacial pace, and I started to wonder whether I'd miss my appointment if I signed in late, but, at last, my turn came, just a few minutes before the scheduled time for my visit with Edna.

I'd thought twice before I'd registered on the detention center's website and requested a time for visitation, but, in the end, my curiosity had won out over my more reasonable impulse to avoid the woman. I couldn't imagine why she wanted to spend one of her two weekly social visits with me. It would make more sense to choose to see a relative or a friend rather than me, the woman who'd discovered her secret past and thus her vulnerability to blackmail.

Finally, I made it to the thick black line painted on the floor in front of the counter. In case someone didn't know what that line meant, "Stand Behind Line until Called" was painted in bold black letters on the floor.

"Next."

I quickly walked to the counter. The clerk didn't even look up.

"Name and ID." It wasn't a question; it was a command.

"Laurel McMillan. Here's my driver's license," I said, sliding it toward her. She glanced at me, just long enough to decide I was who I said I was before returning my license.

"Be advised that your name will be run for outstanding warrants. You're subject to search and expulsion at any time. Sign here."

I signed a statement agreeing to abide by the numerous visitation rules. I promised not to eat or drink, touch the video screen, wear a halter top or a short skirt, wear clothing with offensive messages, or go barefoot.

As soon as I handed the paperwork back to the clerk, she directed me to report to the jail attendant, who was standing by.

"Follow me."

I followed him into a small room lined with lockers. He opened one of them and instructed me to leave my handbag, coat, cell phone, gloves, scarf, and cap inside. I shuddered when I realized that now I had no way of contacting anyone in the outside world.

"This way." I followed the attendant down a short hallway and into a large room that had video monitors, each with a phone next to it, along one wall. I'd seen lots of movies in which visitor and prisoner sat on opposite sides of a glass panel, but here I wouldn't be in the same room with Edna, who would be talking to me from some other part of the building. A sign next to the phone receiver proclaimed that our visit was subject to monitoring. Gingerly, I removed the phone from its hook, the monitor flashed to life, and Edna's face popped up on the screen. She had dark circles under her red-rimmed eyes, and I doubted that she'd slept more than a few hours since her arrest.

"I didn't do it! I didn't kill Matt! You've got to believe me," she said urgently.

"Why does it matter what I believe, Edna?" I asked. "It'll be up to a jury to decide."

"No. No. No. No! It can't get that far. That's why I need you to find out who really did it."

I was so shocked I just sat there with my mouth open for a few moments before I responded.

"I'm not a private investigator. Maybe your lawyer could hire one."

"I can't afford that. I can't even really afford my lawyer, but if you get me off soon, I won't owe him more money."

"Why didn't you ask for a public defender?"

"Hah! Never again. I had one of those once, and he was totally worthless. That's why I ended up with a felony conviction."

"So you never used a dirty needle to inject patients?"

"There were extenuating circumstances," Edna whined. "You don't understand. Anyway, I don't want to talk about that now. We don't have much time. Can't you nose around and figure out who the real killer is?"

"I don't know, Edna. I don't think that's a good idea."

"You *owe* me, Laurel," she said fiercely.

"I don't owe you a thing. I should go. This conversation is a waste of time."

"Wait. Don't go! I'm sorry. I didn't mean that."

"Okay. Edna, convince me that you didn't do it."

"Why would I? I didn't even know that I'd be in the Danielses' house Sunday. Jennifer called me all in a panic early in the morning and said that the agency's nurse had bailed and they couldn't get another nurse in until evening. She offered me five hundred dollars to stay with Matt for the day. She said I wouldn't even have to go upstairs—she knows my own knees aren't so good—because Matt was in the downstairs bedroom to recover, and he wouldn't be able to go upstairs for a while himself."

"Does she know you're not licensed?"

"She didn't care. He wasn't able to get up yet, so all I had to do was keep an eye on him, hand him his pills, fetch whatever he needed, and empty his urine bag. She said she'd help in the morning, but in the afternoon her book club would be there, and I'd be on my own. It seemed easy enough, and the money was good, so I agreed."

"Why did Justin accuse you? He must have had some reason for thinking you'd harm his father."

"Because I had an argument with his father once, but that was five years ago. I didn't hold a grudge."

That didn't sound like the Edna I knew. The argument must have had something to do with the motive that the police and district attorney thought Edna had for murdering her neighbor. I figured I'd be more likely to get the full story from Justin or Jennifer than from Edna, so I let it go.

"At your arraignment, the lawyer from the district attorney's office said they have physical evidence pointing to you. Do you know what it is?"

"Yeah. They brought it up when they tried to question me, but my lawyer told me not to respond, so I didn't say anything. They claim that there were lots of tiny beads in the pockets of the smock I was wearing. They said the beads must have come off Jennifer's peacock pillow when I smashed it into Matt's face. That's not true. I never touched that pillow."

I remembered the white smock Edna had worn that day. It was apron-like with a deep pocket across the front bodice and even deeper pockets in the skirt. It reminded me of something vendors might wear at a farmers' market or a craft fair so they could easily reach their change and other items they might need.

"Why didn't you stay in the bedroom with Matt?"

"I only stepped out for a minute."

"Stepped out where, Edna?"

"If you must know, I was in the restroom." She hesitated, looking down at her hands. "There's an ensuite bathroom directly off the bedroom. You don't have to go out into the hall to get to it."

"So you're saying that while you were in the ensuite, someone came into the room, smothered Matt, and you didn't hear a thing."

"No, I didn't. The bedroom has wall-to-wall carpeting." She sounded annoyed.

"You're positive you never left the bedroom suite?"

Edna nodded vigorously. "I'm positive."

"I don't believe you." I replaced the phone on its hook and started to stand up. I could see Edna wildly gesturing for me to stay, so I sat back down and picked up the phone again.

"Are you going to tell me what really happened?" I didn't wait for her to answer. "Because if not, I'm not wasting any more time here."

"Okay. Okay. I might have gone to the sunroom for a while."

"Might have or did?"

Edna gulped nervously. "Did," she said in a voice so soft I barely heard her.

"How long were you there?"

"Oh, I don't know. Not long."

"Honestly, Edna, talking to you is like pulling teeth. You're the one who claims you're innocent, but, so far,

I'm not convinced."

"All right. I fell asleep in the sunroom. I was reading a magazine, and I dozed off."

"How long were you there?"

"About an hour."

Now, *that* I could believe. I shook my head and put my hand on my forehead, eyes downcast. What in the world had possessed this woman to leave Matt alone in the first place?

"Why did you leave Matt's room, Edna? What if he'd needed something and nobody was there to help him?"

She shrugged. "I knew he wouldn't wake up very soon, not with all the pain medication he was taking, but, just to be sure, I gave him one extra pill."

When she saw the shocked look on my face, she hastened to assure me that one extra pill wasn't enough to hurt Matt. I shook my head, blown away by the incredible carelessness of the woman. Edna hadn't persuaded me that she hadn't smothered Matt. In fact, I could understand the reasons Walker had arrested her. On the other hand, I wasn't really sure that she had killed Matt, despite her negligence.

"Come on, Laurel," she pleaded. "Can't you help me out?"

"I don't know, Edna."

Her face contorted in anger, she said loudly, "That's just like you, Miss Holier-Than-Thou." Then her decibel level went up several notches, and she yelled, "I'm telling you the truth!"

Suddenly the screen in front of me went blank. I imagined that the detention center attendant who monitored the inmates had shut her broadcast down when she started yelling. It was just as well because I was tired of listening to her whining and wheedling. I hung up the phone and left the building as soon as I retrieved my belongings from the locker. I never wanted to return to the dismal detention center, and it wouldn't bother me a bit if I never saw Edna again, either.

Unfortunately, that little bit of nagging doubt about her guilt wouldn't go away although I tried to concentrate on my next task of the day, which was to teach the last class in my perfect pillow series. I had over an hour before class started, so I drove to Cuppa Joe and downed three cups of coffee along with a yummy blueberry muffin.

The minute I stepped into my classroom, I resolved to put Edna out of my mind, but it proved impossible because the gossip from my students constantly reminded me of the murder.

Since this was the final class in my perfect pillows series, I'd asked students to bring a pillow they'd made on their own outside of class so that we could have our own version of show-and-tell before we constructed the last class project, a satin and lace neck roll pillow trimmed with ribbons.

Four students brought pillows to show the class, and I was a bit surprised that Bud was one of them. He'd struggled through most of the classes even with a little help from me and some of his classmates. He had managed to complete the cushions for his patio furniture during class, using one of our industrial sewing machines.

Bud was sitting next to Amy, and I began to wonder whether a romance was budding between them. Widow and widower—they were both alone now, and they were both lonely. On the dance floor, they were a perfect match, and when Bud won our table's centerpiece at the FFF gala, he'd given it to Amy. She loved reading romance novels, and she loved matchmaking. I wondered whether she could be doing some matchmaking for herself. On the other hand, the twenty-year age gap between the two could prove an impediment.

When I asked the students who'd brought a pillow for show-and-tell to pass their pillows around so we could all take a close look at their creations, I couldn't help thinking that if Jennifer were present, she probably would have brought her blue peacock pillow, but now it was sitting in police evidence storage. I shook off thoughts of Matt's murder and tried to concentrate on the class.

Amber produced a pair of cheerful floral piped pillows that she'd made when she entered the bedroom decorating contest. She'd chosen to redecorate her guest room, and as she'd planned when I first announced the contest, she'd sewn the pillows, but purchased the window and bed coverings. Amber's participation in the paint store's contest made me think of Jennifer and our last book club meeting.

Cynthia had rescued an old needlepoint picture of a cute kitten that she'd made years before and never blocked to frame. She'd taken the picture to Nettie's Needlepoint Shoppe and let the pros straighten the canvas before she made it into a pillow.

Amy had made a pillow featuring a large pink fabric bow. The ends of the bow extended across the black-and-white polka dotted pillow and were sewn into the seams. She'd added a matching pink ruffle to the edges. I loved the retro color palette.

We applauded enthusiastically after each presentation. Bud's turn came last. Swooping up a dark green trash bag, he came to the front of the classroom.

"Cynthia recycled her needlework to make her pillow, and I decided to recycle when I made mine, too. Last time I visited my sister, I helped her take some used furniture and clothing to her local charity store.

She had an old brown leather coat that she planned to donate, but when we were bagging it, we noticed some ripped seams. She was going to throw it away, but I salvaged it, and that's what I used to make my pillow. Now you all know how great I am at sewing." This produced laughter from his classmates. "Okay. So I'm not! But then I thought, what if I could make a pillow without sewing a stitch, and that's exactly what I did." Reaching into the bag, he paused rather dramatically and produced his pillow. "Ta Dah!" He'd decorated the brown leather pillow with knotted and tied fringe cut from the same leather, and it looked as though it would be right at home in a room decorated in Southwestern style.

We gave him a round of applause, and he bowed. I congratulated him on his clever idea as he handed the pillow to Cynthia to examine before passing it along to the other students. When he returned to his seat, I noticed that he and Amy had their heads together. I'd have to find out the scoop about their relationship, but that would have to wait until I could talk to her alone.

Show-and-tell had taken a bit longer than I'd anticipated, so I hastily presented the instructions for the lace and satin neck roll pillow, and the students went to work. Luckily it was an easy project, and they worked on their own while I showed Bud how to make a tailored neck roll, using tan suedecloth and a pattern I'd made. Although his neck roll looked a trifle lopsided when he finished it, he seemed satisfied with the result after Amy tugged on it to coax the seams into their proper places.

It didn't look as though I'd have a chance to talk to Amy alone. When class ended, a couple of students remained at the sewing machines to finish their pillows while the others took their time packing up and chatting on the way out. Amy and Bud walked out together, but when I glanced out the window a few minutes later, I noticed that they had gone their separate ways.

"Great class, as usual, Laurel," Cynthia said.

"Thank you. That means a lot coming from you. You're the queen of all things organized and efficient. I like to keep things on track in class, but it doesn't always happen."

"Well, I think you do a great job. The students have such a range of skill levels, but you manage to keep them happy. If you're ready to leave, I'll walk out with you." After we said goodbye to the two remaining students, I put my supplies in my bag and we left the classroom.

"Have you heard anything about the arrangements for Matt's funeral yet?" I asked.

"No, but I have heard from Jennifer. She called me this morning, saying that the police said she and Justin can return home today. Her parents, aunt, and some other relatives are driving in from Chicago today, and they're all going to stay at the house. It'll be good for her to have family with her for support, but, at the same time, having all those relatives stay there makes her a hostess, too. I hope it's not too much for her. Even though she has Katie to help, I thought I'd take a ham over later this afternoon, and Amy's going to make her corn casserole to take, too."

"Good idea. I want to contribute, but since I'm the world's worst cook, I'll pick up some salads at Foster's deli, and maybe Amber can furnish dessert. I'd ask Tracey, but I know she has to work late today."

"That sound fine. I'm sure some of her close neighbors will be bringing food, too."

"Okay, I'll let Amber know."

"See you later."

As I drove out of the community center's parking lot, I thought about the last time Cynthia, Amy, Amber, and I had visited Jennifer's home. It had to be very difficult for Jennifer and Justin to return to the scene of the crime. When my husband had died in a terrible car crash several years ago, I hadn't wanted to go anyplace that reminded me of his loss. Since the entire city of Seattle had reminded me, I'd followed Tracey's suggestion to move, and that's how I'd come to live in Hawkeye Haven.

Matt's was the second murder in our guard-gated community within six months, and it had understandably shocked and rattled the residents, especially because many of them didn't think Edna was guilty. If she wasn't the culprit, then whoever had murdered Matt was still "running around loose," as one of my students had put it.

Tracey and I weren't the only ones who had figured out that it was possible for someone to have entered Jennifer's house, sneaked through the guest powder room into the back hallway, gone into the bedroom where Matt was sleeping, and smothered him. I thought that scenario possible but highly unlikely, which meant that someone already in the home had killed Matt. That group included everybody who'd attended our book club meeting on Sunday—Jennifer, Cynthia, Amy, Amber, Marcie, Tracey, and me—as well as Justin, Bunny, Katie, and Edna.

Even though I'd told Edna I wasn't convinced of her innocence (that was probably the wrong word because she was far from innocent), I didn't feel positive that she was guilty, either.

I might have some DIY detective work to do, after all.

Chapter 7

As soon as I pulled into the garage, Bear began to bark. After I parked and grabbed my supplies, I opened the door to the hallway slowly so that it didn't bump him.

He couldn't wait for mommy to get home. He nuzzled me, ran up and down the hallway, and returned for a pat. When I reached the kitchen, he raced around me, bouncing for joy. He'd been alone for several hours by this time, so I knew he wanted to play.

I left my supplies on the kitchen counter and went out onto the patio with him. Several inches of snow covered the backyard, but not the patio, thanks to the colonel, who had cleared it off with his snow blower after the last big snowstorm.

The colonel had looked a bit forlorn that day. While my next-door neighbor Liz vacationed in Florida, he'd been catsitting for Miss Muffett, Liz's Persian cat, and it was obvious that he missed Liz. They'd met during a Hawkeye Haven homeowners' association meeting when they'd both shown up to protest the former HOA president's high-handed tactics. They'd been an item ever since.

While Liz was enjoying the warm Florida sunshine, the colonel kept himself busy with his new snow blower. He lived in Hawkeye Haven several blocks from our neighborhood, and every time it snowed, he buzzed back and forth, between his block and ours, clearing snow for his neighbors and ours. He'd cleared off my patio several times, saving me from the chore, although usually I just shoveled a narrow path through it if the snow wasn't light and fluffy, rather than clearing the entire patio.

Bear found his hard rubber ball under a forlorn patio chair and brought it to me so that we could play fetch. I threw the ball, and when it plopped into the snow, he dug it out, trotted back to me, and gave it a toss with a whip of his head. I was supposed to catch it, but that seldom happened. Instead, I retrieved it from the patio and threw it out into the backyard for him again. Bear looked cute with snow all over his muzzle. After several repetitions, I felt so cold that I wanted to abandon the game, but Bear's expectant looks each time I picked up the ball to throw for him kept me in the game a while longer. Finally, I couldn't take the cold any longer. My mittens were soaked, and I knew my face was red from exposure. When I turned to slide open the patio door, Bear knew playtime had ended, but in a last-ditch effort for some fun, he galloped back into the yard and rolled in the snow before arriving back at the door, eager and panting for the next thing on his doggie agenda—snacks.

After I toweled him off and put my winter garb in the laundry room to dry, I gave him some peanut butter dog treats and warmed myself with a big mug of coffee. I called Amber to let her know about the food brigade headed to Jennifer's house later, and she agreed to bring an apple pie and some ginger cookies.

While Bear dozed, I wrote instructions for one of the pillow projects that would be in my new book, *DIY Perfect Pillows*. I wanted to talk to both Wes and Tracey, but I didn't like to interrupt them during normal work hours, so I refrained from sending them text messages. I could wait until evening to catch up.

When I glanced at the clock, I noticed that it had taken me longer than I'd anticipated to write the instructions, and I needed to get on the road because Foster's, my favorite supermarket, was located on the other side of town. Even though it wasn't the most convenient store for residents of Hawkeye Haven, Foster's topped my list because I seldom cook, and it has the best deli in Center City.

I considered giving Bear an early dinner, but since I didn't plan to stay long at Jennifer's, I decided to wait until I got home. He looked sadly at me with his big brown eyes when I put my winter coat on, and he whined softly. I found it hard to resist his begging ways, so I dropped a few baby carrots into his bowl to pacify him while I sneaked out of the house.

At Foster's deli counter, the salads all looked good to me, and since I couldn't decide on just one, I selected three: a chicken salad with almonds and cranberries, a Waldorf salad, and a Caesar salad. Then I added some sesame seed rolls from Foster's bakery to my shopping basket, in case someone wanted to make a sandwich with the chicken salad, and a few lemon scones for myself.

Fortified with provisions, I arrived at Jennifer's house and found a parking spot halfway down the block. As I was gathering the Foster's bags from my trunk, a ruddy-faced woman came along.

"Going to the Danielses'?" she asked.

"Yes. You must be a neighbor."

She nodded. "I just dropped off some twice-baked potatoes. It's a good thing, too. Lots of Jennifer's relatives have arrived, and Katie's not coping with the crowd too well. Jennifer has never permitted any disposable serving ware in her house, so Katie has to round up enough china for everyone. I told her I'd bring over an extra set of plates and bowls."

"That's nice of you. If you need some help carrying them, I can come to your house as soon as I drop these salads and rolls off."

"That's sweet of you, dear, but my husband and son can help me bring them over. Such a shame about Matt, but I can't believe Edna had anything to do with it. It's not her fault he died on her watch. Honestly, I don't know what this world's coming to," she said as she shook her head. "Edna lives right down the street, you know," she confided, pointing out Edna's house.

"Well, I'd better get going," I said, shivering as I made my escape. I was afraid that Jennifer's garrulous neighbor would continue chatting while I turned into an icicle.

I was greeted at the door by a gray-haired lady dressed in a burgundy velour track suit.

"Come in out of the cold," she exclaimed. "I'm Jennifer's Aunt Barbara. Just call me Barb."

"Nice to meet you, Barb. I'm Laurel McMillan."

"Let's go back to the kitchen, Laurel. Let me take those bags. What do we have here?"

"Salads and rolls."

"Thank you. We'll put those out in the dining room right away. So many neighbors have brought food. It's very thoughtful. I live in a high-rise in Chicago, and this would never happen there. Say, your name sounds familiar. Aren't you the DIY lady who teaches classes here?" After I acknowledged that I was, she continued, "Jennifer really enjoys your classes."

"That's good to hear, although I don't think Jennifer needs much help. She's a very talented and creative designer. In fact, she recently won two design contests."

"Yes, I know. She was so excited when she told me. Jennifer needs some ego boosting. She sure didn't get any from Matt, but he's gone now, and I shouldn't speak ill of the dead."

She set the bags on the kitchen island's black granite counter and removed the salads and rolls from the

Foster's grocery bags.

"Katie, we need three more serving bowls and a platter. We could use those antique cut-glass bowls that are on the bottom shelf of the china cabinet."

"I'll get them." Katie stooped to open a door in the island and pulled out a large white platter. "For the rolls," she said, as she placed it on the counter.

Katie went to the dining room and returned with the cut-glass bowls, muttering "big fuss for a bad man."

"What did you say, Katie?" Barb asked sharply, but Katie held her ground.

"Big fuss for a bad man. Matt was always talking about charity and how much he gave to charity, but he didn't treat Jennifer very well."

"Calm down, Katie." Barb cautioned.

"I'm sorry,." Katie sniffed, "but it's the truth."

"Well, be that as it may, let's not speak ill of the dead."

"Humph," Katie muttered as she dumped one of the containers of salad into a cut-glass bowl and carried it into the dining room.

Clearly, Katie had not been a fan of her late employer, or at least one of her employers. Since she'd felt upset by Matt's treatment of Jennifer, I supposed she must like her.

"Jennifer's in the living room, Laurel," Barb said, as she arranged the rolls on the platter. "Just a second, and I'll show you."

"That's okay. I know the way, Barb."

"Oh, right. Thanks for bringing these."

I went through the dining room, where a huge ham sat on a sideboard loaded with food. Among the other offerings, I saw Amy's corn casserole, a hearty dish perfect for winter, and Amber's apple pie and ginger cookies, a special favorite of mine. I recognized a few of the people who were sitting around the table eating as residents of Hawkeye Haven because I'd seen them around the community, and I assumed they must be Jennifer's neighbors. I walked through, into the living room, where Jennifer sat on the sofa next to an older woman who looked very much like Jennifer. Cynthia and Amy perched on the loveseat facing them. Murmuring my condolences, I squeezed Jennifer's hand and pulled up a chair.

"Thank you for coming, Laurel." Jennifer looked even paler than usual. I doubted that she'd had much sleep in the last few days.

"Of course."

"This is my mother, Nancy Burgess. Dad's in the den with my sister and brother-in-law and some of the neighbors."

"So nice of you girls to bring food," Nancy said. "Would you like some tea? I know I would. There's nothing like a good strong cup of tea." She turned to her daughter. "You look as though you could do with a cup right about now, too."

I jumped up. "I'll make it," I offered. At least I could make myself useful by brewing and serving the tea. I felt awkward, not knowing what to say to Jennifer. I remembered feeling the same way when my husband died, as friends and relatives had arrived to console me. I hadn't known what to say then, either.

I returned to the kitchen and began to fill the tea kettle, telling Katie, who was taking plates out of the dishwasher and stacking them on the counter, that Mrs. Burgess wanted some tea, and I'd offered to make it.

"Here's the teapot." She reached into the cupboard and brought out a large pink chintz china teapot and a tin of tea. "Jennifer likes this kind."

While the water boiled, I filled a tea infuser ball with Jennifer's preferred blend and put it in the flowery teapot, and Katie produced a large silver tray, setting a small bowl of sugar and a little pitcher of cream on it. She went back to the cupboard and took a delicate pink chintz china cup from its hook.

"How many?"

"Umm. Four." I decided I didn't want any tea. I had planned to drop off the food and stay only a few minutes, but it seemed rude to leave when everybody else was staying. I figured I should probably wait at least half an hour before making my excuses.

While I waited for the tea to steep, I decided to ask Katie if she could confirm Edna's story that she was in the sunroom, rather than in the sickroom the day of Matt's death. After all, the sunroom was only a few steps down the back hallway from the kitchen, and if Katie went to the back of the kitchen, she might have seen Edna.

"Katie, I wonder if you could tell me whether you saw Edna anytime Sunday afternoon."

"Sure. I saw her when she came in here yelling about Matt."

"That's the only time then?"

"Yeah."

"I saw her."

I was so startled that I almost dropped the tea cups that I'd been arranging on the silver tray. I turned to see Bunny, closing the basement door. "I need some more chips for the kids," she said to Katie, not noticing my reaction. "Justin's cousins," she explained. "We're teaching them how to play pool."

"When you say you saw Edna Sunday afternoon, do you mean before we discovered that Matt had died?"

"Yeah, I saw her a couple of times when I came up to get us some beer. I left my purse in the sunroom, and I went in there to get it. The old bat was snoring, if you can believe it," Bunny said.

"And you saw her again later?" I prompted.

"Uh, huh. I couldn't find my phone, and I thought maybe it fell out of my purse. She was still there."

"Do you have any idea how long she may have been there?"

"Not a clue. I guess it was a while, though. Probably at least an hour."

"You told the police, right?"

"The cops? Nope. They asked where I was all afternoon, and I told them Justin and I were in the rec room downstairs, except when we came up to get some food. I guess I forgot about seeing Edna. It doesn't matter, anyway. They've already arrested her."

"I think you really should amend your statement."

"Yeah, well, maybe." Bunny shrugged.

She grabbed a large bag of corn chips and flounced off, slamming the basement door as she left. I wished that I hadn't mentioned the police to her because now she would not only be on her guard if questioned but she'd also probably complain about me to Justin, and then he might not want to talk to me himself. I knew today wasn't the time to ask Jennifer about Matt's long-ago argument with Edna, but I thought I might persuade Justin to tell me what he knew about it. Just as I was thinking that didn't seem likely now, the basement door popped open, and Justin burst into the kitchen.

"Bunny forgot the salsa," he explained, ducking into the refrigerator and rummaging around. He frowned. "I don't see any. Katie, are we out of salsa already?"

"There's some out in the car. I've been too busy to bring in all the groceries," she muttered. "Just wait a second, and I'll go get the salsa."

"Same old Katie. She wouldn't go down to the basement if her life depended on it. Superstitious," he said.

I saw my opening and I took it. Obviously, Bunny hadn't had a chance to tell Justin about our conversation.

"Justin, I wonder whether I could ask you something."

"Shoot."

"Well, it's about Edna."

"All I can say about her is that I'm glad the cops didn't waste any time locking her up."

"Yes, her arrest came very quickly. You mentioned that she had a motive, but I guess the neighbors were shocked because they couldn't believe someone they knew would harm your father."

"What I couldn't believe was that mom actually hired her to take care of dad. He wasn't too happy about it, but he wasn't in any position to object. Anyway, he was taking so many painkillers that he slept most of the time, so I didn't insist on making other arrangements. If I had, dad would still be with us. It's my fault he's dead."

He sounded so forlorn I would have given him a hug right there if I'd known Justin better, but we'd never been formally introduced, and I wasn't sure he even knew who I was. Of course, he'd seen me Sunday, so he must realize I was a book club member.

"It's not your fault. You shouldn't blame yourself, Justin. You couldn't have known what was going to happen."

"Yeah. I suppose you're right."

"Why do you think Edna did it?" I was pushing my luck, but I hoped he'd tell me.

"She and dad had a big blow-up about five years ago, and they haven't spoken since."

"You don't happen to know what their argument was about, do you?"

"Something about her son."

"Oh, I didn't know she had a son."

"Uh, huh. He's in Fort Madison now."

"He's in the army?"

"No. Fort Madison's a town, the town where the state penitentiary is."

"What? You mean he's an inmate?"

"Yep. He's a lifer."

Chapter 8

Whoa! Edna had never mentioned a son, let alone one serving a life sentence in prison. That fact still didn't explain the reason for Edna's years-old argument with Matt. I'd need to find out the reason for their dispute from someone else because Justin evidently didn't have the full story—only enough to be convinced that Edna held such a deep grudge against his father that she'd smothered him. Justin could be right. Lieutenant Walker certainly thought so, and so did the district attorney, which meant that, as far as they were concerned, the murderer was housed in the county detention center, and they didn't need to consider any other suspects. On the other hand, I wasn't so sure. I'd told Edna she hadn't convinced me of her innocence, but neither was I convinced of her guilt. I just didn't know.

After I served tea to Jennifer, her mother, Cynthia, and Amy, I lingered a few moments out of politeness, but when Cynthia and Amy rose to leave, I took the opportunity of bowing out with them.

The minute I reached home, Bear raised a mighty racket. It was an hour past his usual dinnertime, and he wanted to let me know it. As I prepared his meal, he danced around excitedly. When I set his bowl down on his mat, he wolfed it down as usual, before turning to his water bowl and slurping noisily. A happy canine camper once again, he wagged his tail and sat beside me while I petted him. I told him he was a good boy, although not a very patient one.

Driving home from Jennifer's, I'd considered calling Wes to find out whether he'd be free to go out to dinner, but now that I was home, I didn't feel much like braving the cold again. The temperature, which had been dropping steadily all day, was around zero now. Just as I turned on the gas fireplace in the den, my phone rang. It was Wes, wanting to know if I'd like to go out to dinner. When I suggested a take-out pizza at my house, he offered to pick it up on his way over, and I told him I'd call in our order to the Pizza Palace.

"I'll have to come back to work later this evening, though," he said.

"Not again!"

"I'm afraid so. On top of the cold case we've been working, we caught another new case this morning."

No wonder I hadn't heard from him all day.

"We already know who the perp in this new case is, but we need to wrap up some loose ends tonight."

"Well, I'm sorry you're going to have to go out in the cold twice then. It's like Antarctica out there."

"You mean Iowa in winter?"

"You got it."

After I ordered our pizza, I pre-heated the oven and set plates on the counter next to it and napkins on the dining room table. Assuming that Wes probably wouldn't want a beer since he had to return to work, I checked my supply of sodas. I also brewed some coffee. Wes might need some extra caffeine for the long night ahead since he had to return to work.

Bear must have heard Wes closing his car door when he arrived because he ran to the door and barked. I opened the door before he had a chance to ring the bell, and he blew in. At least, it seemed that way with an icy wind at his back. Bear managed to insert himself between Wes and me, and we had to laugh at the dog's antics as Wes handed me the pizza box and gave Bear a tummy rub while I went to the kitchen to slip the pizza into the oven to warm.

After a few minutes, man and dog trailed into the kitchen, and Wes gave me a hug while Bear bounced around us.

Wes's red face attested to the bitter cold outside, and I was glad to be staying home for dinner and sorry that Wes had to face the frosty air again later.

"It shouldn't take too long to heat the pizza. What would you like to drink? I have beer, soda, coffee."

"Some coffee right now would be great, and maybe a soda with the pizza. I'd like to have a beer, but duty calls."

"I thought you might say that," I said, as I filled a mug and handed him his coffee. "Do you think spring will ever get here?"

"It can't come soon enough for me. This miserable weather! I should have booked February in Hawaii for us instead of June on the Mississippi."

"Hawaii sounds very inviting right about now. But you're swamped with work! The department should hire a few more detectives and give you a break."

"I wish. The city just went through a round of budget cuts, and now they're talking about even more, so it doesn't look like we're going to be getting any new hires anytime soon, and promotions have been frozen."

"Oh, no!"

"Same old, same old." He shrugged. "It happens periodically. Seriously, though, Laurel, I don't expect my workload to lighten anytime soon. You've been very understanding about all the postponed dates." He frowned. "I hope it's not going to cause a problem for us."

"Of course not. I knew what your hours were like when we first started dating. It's disappointing when we have to cancel our plans, but we make up for it later." I winked and smiled at him. "Seriously, it's not a problem."

Wes looked relieved. I was surprised that he still thought his schedule might become an issue in our relationship. I'd never had such thoughts myself, but this wasn't the first time he'd brought it up.

The timer bell on the oven beeped, startling me.

"Pizza time."

Wes loaded his plate while I settled for a couple of slices. We carried our plates to the table, and Bear followed us. When we sat down, Bear sat too. Then he held his front paws up under his chin to beg for a morsel. He looked so cute I couldn't resist, but I had no intention of giving him spicy pizza. Knowing his tricks, I'd come prepared, and I pulled one of his pumpkin treats out of my pocket and gave it to him.

"Lie down now, Bear," I said, and he complied. "Good boy."

Wes grinned. "That dog has you wrapped around his big paw."

"Don't I know it."

"We haven't really had a chance to talk since we went to Tony's for dinner, so tell me, did you go to Edna's arraignment?"

"I did, and she saw me there. She looked right at me, and afterwards her lawyer delivered a message that she wanted to see me."

"Oh, no. Don't tell me you visited her at the detention center."

"This morning. It's the dreariest place I've ever seen. I won't be visiting again; that's for sure."

"I'm all ears. Why did she want to see you?"

"She said she's innocent, and that I should find out who really killed Matt." I related our conversation while Wes munched on his pizza. "I don't know what to think, Wes. She said that she gave Matt more pain medication than his doctor prescribed, and I can't think of any reason she'd admit that, so I tend to believe that part of her story. Edna fibs so readily it's difficult to know what the truth is. Because I can't fathom her motive, I have some doubt about her guilt—and, by that, I mean Matt's murder—because she's guilty of negligence, if nothing else."

"That she is, although I don't know if her negligence is actionable. I'm not sure the district attorney would charge her in a case like this, and if the family filed a civil suit, the lawyers, judge, and jury would have to sort out the mess. Was she doing a favor for a neighbor, or did she represent herself as a licensed nurse to Jennifer?"

"Hmm. I see what you mean. When I asked Edna if Jennifer knew she'd lost her nursing license, Edna claimed Jennifer didn't care. I find that hard to believe. It's far more likely that Jennifer didn't even question her status because everybody who knows Edna knows she used to be a nurse. What if it's true, though? We know Matt wasn't always very nice to his wife. Maybe she had more of a reason to want Matt dead than Edna did."

"Welcome to my world. Witnesses and accused perpetrators often try to misdirect an investigation, hedge, or lie when we question them. In a case like this, spouses come under intense scrutiny because, statistically, they're more likely to have done the deed."

"Jennifer left the book club meeting for a few minutes, probably long enough to smother Matt, but then again, anybody in the house could have done it, or some other person could have come in and done it."

"How so?"

"Just a sec." I went to the office and grabbed a pen and piece of printer paper. Returning to the dining room, I drew a diagram of the floor plan of Jennifer's house and explained the path through the guest powder room that someone from outside could have taken to enter Matt's bedroom."

"Okay. I'll grant you that it's possible, but I'd also have to say I find that scenario highly unlikely. The perp would have to enter just at the right time, when you were all in the dining room or kitchen, and there's no way anyone outside the house could have known that without communicating with an insider." Wes paused. "Unless the insider was Edna, the perp would have had to deal with her as well as with Matt. I just don't buy it."

"That's what I thought, too. It's a long shot at best. If Edna didn't do it, I guess that puts me back in the frame. I was there."

"Nope. You're in the clear along with Cynthia and Tracey. All three of you were with someone else during the entire afternoon, according to what you told me Sunday night. Remember?"

"Um, hmm. That's true. So that only leaves . . . let's see," I said, mentally tallying the occupants of Jennifer's house Sunday afternoon, "Jennifer, Amy, Amber, Marcie, Katie, Justin, Bunny, and Edna, but what I keep coming back to is that Edna doesn't seem to have a solid motive to kill Matt, but then again, neither do the others, as far as I know. Even though Jennifer did a couple things that seemed odd, I can't picture her smothering Matt with her prize-winning pillow. It meant a lot to her, even if Matt didn't, and her feelings for Matt aren't a certainty, either. She seemed genuinely shocked when we found him."

"Well, it's all speculation, but even though Walker jumps to conclusions occasionally—and you didn't hear that from me, by the way—I think he'll get it sorted out eventually. The district attorney insists on having all the i's dotted and the t's crossed before taking a case to trial, so just because Edna's been charged doesn't mean Walker has stopped investigating."

"I get that. Oh, I almost forgot! A bunch of us, Jennifer's friends and neighbors, took food to the house this afternoon, and Bunny—you remember Bunny? She was with Justin the night of the gala."

"Uh, huh, Hard to forget."

"Anyway, Bunny happened to tell me that she saw Edna sleeping in the sunroom that afternoon for at least an hour. She claims she forgot about it, so I'm pretty sure Lieutenant Walker doesn't know. I told her she should tell the police."

"Hearing that puts me in a somewhat awkward position with Walker. I hate to step on his toes."

"I'm sorry."

Wes took my hand and gently squeezed it. "It's all right, sweetheart. You did the right thing in telling me, and I'll pass it along. She'll need to amend her statement. It doesn't prove that Edna's not the culprit, though."

"Yes, I realize that, but it confirms that part of Edna's story."

"True."

"There's more. Justin told me that the argument Edna had with his father concerned Edna's son, who's now serving a life sentence in the state prison."

"That's interesting, but it may not bear on the case at hand, either. Remind me: what's Edna's last name?"

"Elkins. Why?"

"I thought maybe I'd remember something about her son's case, assuming he committed his crime here in Center City, but the name doesn't ring a bell. He may have a different last name, though."

"Would Lieutenant Walker know?"

"He might, but it's not a good idea for me to ask him. Walker won't appreciate me butting into the case, especially after I tell him about Bunny's statement."

"What about Smith? Maybe she'd tell you if she knows."

A strange expression came over Wes's face. He looked both embarrassed and flustered.

"What is it?" I asked.

"Uh . . ."

"You were partners for a long time."

"Yes, but . . . "

"Come to think about it, you never told me why you're not partners anymore. Did you two have a falling out? She's not the easiest person to be around. She hated me from the second you two knocked on my door six months ago. Do you remember?"

"How could I forget? I don't meet a gorgeous redhead every day."

I giggled like a teenager. "Thank you, kind sir."

"As for Smith . . ."

"You always said she's a good detective."

"Yes, but . . ."

"Out with it, Wes. What is it you're not telling me?"

"Okay, but you're not going to like it, and you have to believe me when I tell you I did absolutely nothing to encourage her. I've always thought of her as a colleague, nothing more, but I guess she had other ideas. The reason I asked to change partners is that Smith told me she's in love with me."

Chapter 9

"Wh . . .what?" I stammered. "You're kidding!"

"I'm afraid not."

"Well, I'll say this for her: she definitely has good taste in men." Had I been talking with Tracey, I would have added "if not in anything else," along with my version of a caterwauling "meow," but I didn't think Wes would appreciate it, so I restrained myself.

"So you're not mad?" Wes looked at me hopefully.

"Of course not. How can I blame you for being such a sweetie that she fell for you when I did the same? I'm surprised, but just because I never saw her softer side doesn't mean she doesn't have one."

"When she told me, I was so shocked that I was literally speechless. I'd never noticed that she had a softer side, as you put it. She always acts tough, kind of like she's trying to be one of the guys, but when I told her I didn't feel the same about her, she started crying." Wes looked distressed. "It was awful."

"Did she ask to change partners?"

"No, I did. I made the request to the captain, and he approved it even though I didn't tell him the reason. If that got around the squad room, neither one of us would ever hear the end of it. Luckily, the captain shuffled other personnel at the same time, and there was some grumbling about changing partners, but nobody second-guesses the captain, so that was that. Anyway, now you know why I don't really want to talk to her, let alone ask whether she remembers anything about Edna's son."

I nodded.

"I'll do some checking on my own, without involving Walker or Smith, and I'll let you know any information I find in public records, but let's please let it end there. If Edna didn't smother Matt and the real killer gets wind of your investigating the case, you could be in danger. Does anybody else know you visited Edna at the detention center?"

"No. I haven't even told Tracey. She would never betray a confidence, though."

"I know she wouldn't, not intentionally, but I wish you wouldn't tell her about it right now, and I wish you wouldn't try to question anybody else."

"But I haven't, not really," I protested. "All I did was talk to Justin and Bunny."

"And ask them pointed questions."

"Well, all right, but they didn't mind. Neither one of them was upset."

"Just keep in mind that if Edna isn't the killer, then the real killer is someone you know. Don't do anything to put yourself in danger."

"I won't. I'm not going to confront anyone." That didn't mean I might not talk to people, but I'd learned my lesson about confrontation when I'd snooped around the community following the murder of Victor Eberhart, the former president of Hawkeye Haven's homeowners' association. I hadn't figured out who the killer was until almost the last moment, when he grabbed me and held me at knife point. If it hadn't been for my friends showing up when they did, I might not have survived that ordeal. "Besides, I figure there's a good chance that the right person's already in jail."

"Let's hope so. Say, is there any pizza left?"

"Coming right up."

After Wes left, I turned on the TV to catch the local ten o'clock news, which consisted mainly of reporting about the frigid temperature and its effect on pipes, people, and animals. When a reporter interviewed a Center City resident who'd returned from vacation to find a pipe had burst, flooding his home, I cringed. How awful! I thought about Liz's house, but I knew that the colonel kept a watchful eye on it. He fed Miss Muffet twice a day, but I noticed he checked on the house several times a day, too. After several stories warning people of the dangers of extreme cold and admonishing them not to leave their pets outside in below-zero weather, the official weather report came on, and I was disappointed to hear that we could expect more of the same tomorrow. *Temperatures this cold were just downright scary,* I thought, as I let Bear outside one last time before we went to bed and told him to hurry. Even though Bear likes cold weather, he didn't linger, and I supposed the biting wind and bitter wintry temperature were too much, even for him.

Bear had the same reaction the next morning when I let him out. Since there was no way I'd consider taking him for a walk when it was so cold, I was happy that he seemed content to stay inside because that's exactly what I planned to do.

After he gobbled his breakfast, he flopped down on his bed in my office and soon fell asleep while I worked on some project instructions for my *DIY Perfect Pillows* book. I'd almost completed the instructions when loud, tapping noises interrupted my concentration. I'd kept the blinds closed to help keep out the cold, so I gently pushed the slats apart to find out what was causing the racket. I recognized Colonel Gable from his posture because I couldn't see his face, which was covered with a ski mask. Dressed head to toe in gear fit for an excursion in Antarctica, he was chipping away at ice around Liz's front door with some kind of a metal tool that looked like a spear.

I went to my front door and called to him, beckoning him to come to my house. He left his spear by Liz's door and took the driest route to my house, staying on the sidewalks all the way and removing his ski mask when he arrived at my door.

"Hi, Laurel. Can I help you with something?"

"Come in!" I backed away from the door as he entered and closed it firmly. "Brrr! It's so cold out there I don't know how you stand it. Won't you join me for some coffee?"

"Thanks, Laurel. Don't mind if I do."

As soon as Bear saw the colonel, he sat and extended his paw. The colonel leaned down and solemnly shook hand to paw. Ever since the first time we'd met the colonel, he and Bear had performed the same ritual.

"You're a fine fellow, aren't you, Bear?"

Bear began panting as though he were in full agreement with the colonel's assessment. Of course, I knew better. As usual, my lovable Lab was angling for a hand-out.

"Let's go into the kitchen, and I'll make a fresh pot."

The three of us adjourned to the kitchen where I cranked up my fancy new coffee brewer and popped the lemon scones I'd bought at Foster's bakery into the oven to warm. In the meantime, the colonel had shed his coat, wool scarf, and insulated gloves, putting them on the sofa in the den along with his ski mask.

As soon as the coffee was ready, I poured us both a mug. I knew the colonel always took his coffee black, as I often did, so I skipped offering sugar or milk. Rounding the island that separated my kitchen from the den, I set both mugs down on wool mug rugs on an end table. I grabbed the plate of warmed scones from the island and set them down next to our mugs. Bear eyed the scones, but I pacified him with a peanut butter treat and told him to lie down, which he promptly did, right on the cold tile floor. I'd have opted for his cushy bed next to the fireplace myself, but he seemed perfectly content.

"Careful. It's pretty hot," I warned the colonel.

"Thank you, Laurel," the colonel said, sipping his coffee cautiously. "Hot, but very good. I haven't been outside too long today, but the wind chill is awful. Even wearing all these winter clothes, I can feel the cold to my bones."

"I can't wait for spring myself. It'll be great to have some warm weather and see some grass and flowers when I look outside, instead of snow. Liz'll be coming back from Florida then, too."

"I have good news for you on that score. Liz is coming home Sunday! She heard about the thaw we're due starting tomorrow, and she said she misses everybody here."

"Great! Is she flying into Des Moines?"

"No. She couldn't get a nonstop flight to Des Moines from Miami. I'll pick her up at the airport in Omaha. It's an easy drive over there, once I get on Interstate 80. Her flight's due around twelve-thirty, so I thought we could go to lunch there at a steakhouse we like before we get on the road to come home."

"That sounds good. Would you like me to check on Miss Muffett while you're gone?"

"Yes. That would be a load off my mind. Liz sets such store by Miss Muffett. You have a key to Liz's house, don't you?"

"Sure do, and don't worry about Miss Muffett. If Liz's flight's delayed, just call or text me, and I can give kitty her dinner, too, if need be."

"All right. I really hope it's on time," the colonel said with an almost dreamy, most-uncolonel-like look on his face as he helped himself to a scone.

"You heard about Matt Daniels, I suppose."

"Yes. I didn't know him myself, but I recognized his name, because my gardener, Hank, worked for him, too, and Hank mentioned him a few times. He didn't have much use for the man, I'm afraid. I seem to recall that Hank's wife was Matt's cook."

"Is her name Katie?"

"That sounds right. I'm not sure. It's been quite a while since Hank worked for me. When I first moved in here, I had big plans for my lawn and garden, but I found I didn't have much of a green thumb. My neighbor recommended Hank, and he accomplished wonders."

"You have a beautiful yard."

"Thank you. Now I do, although it looked even better when Hank was tending to it. A couple of years back, he got sick and had to give up his landscaping business. I have another fellow now, but he doesn't quite have Hank's magic touch. I guess I'd call Hank a plant whisperer. I was hoping he'd be able to return to work, but I haven't heard from him."

"That's too bad. I didn't realize Katie's husband was ill."

"A real shame." The colonel sighed and reached for another scone. "From the newspaper account, I gathered that Daniels' nurse was responsible for his death."

"The police think so."

"Do I hear a 'but' there?"

"Maybe. I was there when it happened. Matt's wife Jennifer was holding our monthly book club meeting at their house. Matt's son accused Edna—she's their neighbor, too—of killing his father, and, sure enough, the police arrested her right there at the house. It just seems to me that she has no motive for wanting to harm Matt, but I don't know all the details."

"The paper reported that she lost her nursing license

in another state, so I assume Daniels' death was somehow due to her negligence. If that's the case, maybe she doesn't have a motive. Perhaps she's just a bad nurse."

"Yes, a bad nurse. I do believe that's so." I didn't think I should share what I knew about the cause of Matt's death. It hadn't come out at Edna's arraignment, so I decided to keep mum. "I hope the coffee's warming you up a little, colonel. Would you like some more?"

"That would be great, Laurel," he said, handing me his empty mug. "Then I should get back to work. I want to make sure there aren't any little pieces of ice around Liz's front door or on the sidewalk. It would be all too easy to slip, and, at our age, a fall could cause a broken bone, which can lead to all sorts of complications. That's what happened to my sister who lives in Cedar Rapids a few years ago. She spent two months in the hospital recuperating."

"That's terrible. I'm glad she recovered, and I'm happy you're looking out for Liz."

"Luke helps, too. When Liz told him she was going to Florida for the winter, he promised to have the rover drive by her house more frequently to make sure everything looked in order."

Luke, Liz's long-lost grandson held the post of Chief of Security for Hawkeye Haven. Liz hadn't known that she had a grandson until last year, and she'd feared he wouldn't want to have anything to do with her, but, as it turned out, he was thrilled to learn that his grandmother lives right here in Hawkeye Haven.

"Well, I'd better shove off," the colonel said, rising and putting on his winter garb. "Thank you for the coffee and scones. They really hit the spot." When he pulled his black ski mask over his head, Bear looked askance at him and yelped. "Uh, oh. Bear doesn't like my mask. I'll put it on outside." As soon as the colonel removed the knit mask, Bear, now satisfied with the colonel's appearance, wagged his tail and trailed behind us to the front door.

After the colonel departed, I wasted no time closing the door to keep the bone-chilling cold at bay. The colonel had mentioned a thaw, so I guessed that the weather forecast had changed drastically since I last watched the news. I tapped the weather icon on my smartphone to check and was pleased to learn that a front was due to move in during the night and that, by morning, temperatures would shoot up considerably. That was good news. Not only would I be able to take Bear for a walk without freezing, but it also seemed to me that tomorrow might be a good day for an excursion, perhaps lunch with Cynthia and Amy. The more I thought about it, the more I liked the idea. We'd all been wanting to try the new restaurant tucked away in Sutton Place, Center City's only boutique hotel, but the weather had been so awful the last few weeks that none of us had felt motivated to try it. The hotel's owner had recently renovated a century-old, small brick hotel in downtown Center City, and its restaurant had garnered rave reviews from the local press.

First, I called Cynthia and then Amy, and they both agreed that tomorrow sounded like an excellent day for an outing. Cynthia volunteered to drive, saying that she knew of a good place to park on a side street near the hotel. Pleased at the thought of our ladies' lunch, I was about to return to the project instructions I'd been writing before my visit with the colonel when my phone rang. I picked it up, expecting to see a callback from Cynthia or Amy, but I was surprised to see Wes's face pop up. Wes seldom called me during his workday although he sometimes texted.

"Sweetheart, I'm going to make this quick. I have only a few minutes,"

"What's up?"

"Bad news, I'm afraid. Dad had a heart attack!"

"Oh, no! Wes, I'm so sorry." I hesitated to ask whether or not he had survived. In any case, I couldn't put it that way. I felt tongue-tied, but Wes continued, sparing me from asking the terrible question.

"He's hanging in there, but it sounds serious. Mom's beside herself. She was so upset we couldn't find out much. Denise managed to snag us reservations on the only nonstop flight out of Des Moines to Phoenix today. Jack is going to drive us to the airport."

"Do you need some help packing? I can be at your apartment in less than ten minutes," I said, heading toward my hall closet. I thought about Wes's father, a robust seventy-five-year-old whose lively, engaging manner had charmed me when we'd met for the first time. Wes's parents and his son Derek, a medical student at Johns Hopkins, had all visited at Christmas, and I had joined them for their holiday celebrations at Wes's sister's home. At the time, I already knew Wes's sister Denise and her husband Jack, but I'd been a bit anxious about meeting his parents and son. Thankfully, they'd all welcomed me and put me at ease. We'd had a lovely holiday together. I sincerely hoped this past Christmas wouldn't be Wes's father's last.

"No, all done. I stuffed a few things into a carry-on, and Denise isn't taking any luggage to check, either. We're cutting it very close to board this flight. We should make it just in time, as long as the security check-in line isn't too long. I'm in the foyer right now, waiting for Denise and Jack to show up. Oh, here they are now. Gotta run. I'll call you from the airport if there's time before we board the flight."

"Please keep me posted. I'm so worried."

"You and me both."

Chapter 10

Stunned, I set my phone aside, sank down on the sofa in the den, and buried my face in my hands. Wes and Denise must feel extremely frustrated not to be able to rush to their father's bedside. If they arrived at the airport in Des Moines in time to catch their flight, it would still be several hours before they'd be able to be with their dad and learn more about his condition. The senior Wessons had lived in Center City most of their lives, but after they retired, they began to long for warmer weather, and they decided to move to Phoenix, where Chuck Wesson could play golf year round, and Carolyn Wesson, Wes's mother, could socialize with her sister, who lived in Scottsdale. When I'd met them at Christmas, they'd both talked enthusiastically about their life in Phoenix, so I knew they loved it there.

Sensing my anxiety, Bear lay his head on my lap while I stroked his silky fur. When Wes hadn't called after a couple of hours, I figured he and his sister must have arrived at the airport in time to board their flight. I returned to writing my pillow project instructions, but I had difficulty concentrating and found that it was taking me twice as long as usual. I persevered, though, mainly because I needed to finish my book by the deadline set by my publisher, and I didn't feel like distracting myself by running errands because of the icy cold weather.

Finally, Wes texted, "Just landed. Will call you from hospital."

Knowing they'd arrived in Phoenix made me feel

slightly better, but I was still on pins and needles with worry about Chuck Wesson's condition. All I could do was wait for Wes's call. I busied myself with some household chores. Doing the laundry and cleaning the bathrooms didn't make the time go any faster, but at least I was accomplishing something that needed to be done.

When the phone finally rang, it wasn't Wes.

"This is Brittany Farber from Anderson and Patton Law Offices. May I speak to Laurel McMillan please?"

Law offices? Now what? I didn't know any lawyers, except my own. Then I thought of Edna's lawyer, but I only recalled that he asked me to call him Nate. Anyway, I doubted he would contact me.

"This is Laurel."

"I'm calling for Mrs. Patton, and I apologize for the short notice, but she's reading Matt Daniels' will at ten o'clock tomorrow morning, here in her office, and she's requesting that you attend, if possible."

"Me? But why? I hardly knew the man. This must be a mistake."

"No mistake, Ms. McMillan. Everyone who's named in the will has been asked to come. However, there's no legal requirement that you do so. It's entirely up to you. If you're not able to attend, we'll notify you of the pertinent facts."

"Well, all right," I said, my curiosity aroused. "I'll be there. Where's your office located?"

Brittany gave me the address of the law offices and told me parking was available in the lot in back of the building. I recognized the name of the street as one that ran through downtown Center City. Because Sutton Place was downtown, too, and we'd planned to lunch in the restaurant there at noon, I decided I might as well stay downtown after the reading and meet Cynthia and Amy at the hotel. Since I wouldn't be riding with

Cynthia and Amy, I texted Cynthia to let her know that she didn't need to pick me up.

Briefly, I considered checking with Jennifer to find out whether she knew the reason I'd been invited to the reading of Matt's will, but I decided against it. She already had enough on her plate—the untimely death of her husband, the fact that it had been declared a murder, and a houseful of relatives. I hadn't heard anything about funeral plans yet, so I assumed that the medical examiner's office hadn't yet released Matt's body to the funeral home. Now, in addition to contending with all that, Jennifer had to attend the reading of Matt's will. Of course, Brittany had said attendance wasn't required, but I assumed that Jennifer would be Matt's primary heir, so I thought it very likely that I'd see her in the lawyer's office tomorrow. Even if I did ask her why I'd been summoned, she might not know. I'd just have to wait until tomorrow to satisfy my curiosity.

I had no intention of waiting any longer to find out about Wes's father's condition, though. Despite Wes's assurance that he'd call me when he had news, I decided to call him, but when I called, I was sent straight to voice mail. Wes had his phone turned off, so I left him a brief message.

Shortly after I fed Bear his dinner, he finally called.

"Wes, how is he?" I said, before Wes had a chance to say anything.

"He's hanging in there." Wes sounded exhausted. "He's in a special cardiac care unit, where he's monitored closely, but we weren't able to talk to his doctor until just a few minutes ago. The good news is the doctor's cautiously optimistic about his chances for recovery. The bad news is that they're recommending surgery, something about a blockage. You know me: I'm terrible with medical stuff, but Denise took it all in. Now we're waiting for the surgeon to stop by. I guess they want to operate first thing in the morning. My poor mother looks like she's been through the mill. She hasn't had a thing to eat all day, but she's been drinking coffee like it's going out of style, and she's really wired at this point. After we talk to the surgeon, Denise is going to take her home and try to get her to eat something. They can come back in the morning."

"It sounds as though your dad's getting good care."

"Yes. There's quite a team of nurses in the cardiac unit. I just wish his condition didn't require surgery."

"Oh, Wes. I'm so sorry. Have you been able to talk to your dad?"

"Yes. He's in fairly good spirits, considering. He's scared but trying not to show it."

I could hear Denise calling Wes in the background. "Be right there," he told her. "Looks like the surgeon's here. Gotta run. I'll keep you posted."

I'd hoped for better news, but the doctor's words, "cautiously optimistic," cheered me somewhat, especially when I focused on "optimistic," rather than on "cautiously." Wes called again after talking with the surgeon, and he seemed encouraged, although he insisted on spending the night at the hospital. I didn't try to convince him to go home with his mom and sister because I figured he needed to observe the vigil for his own peace of mind. The surgeon had scheduled the operation for seven the next morning, so with the time difference between Phoenix and Center City, that meant it wouldn't happen until eight Iowa time. Most likely I'd be at the reading of Matt's will when Chuck Wesson came out of surgery. I told Wes I had to attend a meeting the following morning, but I didn't tell him its purpose. There'd be plenty of time for that later. Instead, I told him to call me anytime.

The next morning, I pulled on my winter jacket and stepped outside, onto the patio, when I let Bear out. I held my arms up and embraced the warmer air. Okay, so it wasn't *that* warm, but after the below-zero temperatures we'd been experiencing, thirty degrees almost seemed like a heat wave. Bear bounced around in the snow enthusiastically and ran back to me. He looked up at me with his big brown eyes, and I knew exactly what he wanted—an early morning walk. I decided to oblige him and even promised him a longer walk later in the afternoon. It would be nice to get back to our routine, instead of confining ourselves to the house.

In celebration, I decided to dress up a bit for the meeting and lunch with Amy and Cynthia. Before I showered, I plugged my phone into its charger. I didn't want to chance missing a call or text from Wes. I selected a turquoise blue tunic, a brown pencil skirt, and brown tights to wear along with a brown wool cape and brown waterproof boots. I'd searched far and wide for waterproof boots that looked sleek and stylish, and I'd finally succeeded in finding a pair. I chose a long chain necklace with a wire-wrapped zebra jasper pendant that looked good with the tunic. When I tried my brown cape on, it entirely covered the blue tunic, and I wasn't satisfied with my monochromatic look, so I draped a colorful turquoise print scarf over the cape and added some turquoise stone chandelier earrings. Much better, I decided, as I gazed at my reflection in the mirror. I'd even managed to tame my shoulder-length red hair, which fell in soft waves.

Bear hung around me and cast a suspicious eye as I picked up my purse and grabbed my car keys. He came over to me and rubbed his body against my cape, in an almost cat-like maneuver, his latest method of guilt-tripping me. I petted him gently and told him to be a good boy as I eased open the hall doorway to the garage. He'd deposited some of his chocolate brown fur on my cape, and although it was a color match, I didn't relish the idea of taking it along with me. Luckily, I keep a lint roller and garment brush in my car for just such occasions, and I made quick work of removing Bear's fur before I left the garage.

Heading downtown, I hummed along with music on the radio and tried to remain optimistic about Chuck Wesson's surgery. Because I'd been so worried about Wes's dad's health, I hadn't thought much more about the reading of Matt's will, but as I approached downtown, I couldn't help wondering once again why I'd been invited to attend. I discovered that the Anderson and Patton Law Offices occupied an old two-story Victorian house on a block of similar houses that had all been renovated and converted into offices. The house had been painted dark slate blue with dove gray trim, and a handsome sign outside bore the name of the firm. I spotted a smaller, more discreet sign with an arrow indicating a parking lot behind the building. I turned into the lane and drove around the house. A huge pile of dirty snow occupied one corner of the small parking lot, but the rest of the lot had been plowed. Little rivulets of water from the melting snow pile snaked across the cement, and I was glad I'd worn my waterproof boots. A back entrance to the building opened into a spacious reception area, spanning the space between the front and back entrances, so I didn't have to go around by the lane to enter the front door. From the looks of the reception room, I guessed that the attorneys had gutted the entire building before transforming it into their offices. A wide circular counter occupied the space in the center of the room, and several plush leather sofas and chairs were scattered throughout the room. Two clerks sat behind the counter: a twenty-something man with his sleeves rolled up, who wore pleated trousers attached to wide suspenders, and a smartly dressed woman about my age. I approached the counter and introduced myself.

"Oh, yes, Ms. McMillan. It looks as though you're the first to arrive. Please have a seat. As soon as everybody else gets here, I'll take you all upstairs to Mrs. Patton's office. Would you like a cup of coffee while you wait?"

"No, thanks. I've probably had too much already this morning."

I sat in the corner of one of the sofas near the back door and paged through a fashion magazine for a few minutes until I heard voices outside. I looked up as Justin swung the door open and held it while Katie, Jennifer, Jennifer's mother Nancy, and Bunny filed in ahead of him.

When Jennifer saw me, she stopped so abruptly that her mother almost ran into her.

"What in the world are *you* doing here?" she asked fiercely.

Chapter 11

"I don't really know myself," I said, taken aback. "They called and asked me to come. I have no idea why."

Nancy Burgess frowned slightly and took Jennifer's arm, drawing her aside. While the two were whispering, Marcie came in through the front entrance, smartphone to her ear. Everyone turned to stare at her, and she quickly ended her conversation and said a pleasant "hello" to the group.

"Oh, I . . . I . . . ," Jennifer stammered, looking back and forth from Marcie to me. "I'm sorry, Laurel. I don't know what got into me. I assume Matt must have made a codicil with a bequest to Food for Families."

"Oh, maybe so," I said, although, in my opinion, that still didn't explain why I should be called to the reading. Marcie was the founder of FFF and president of its board of directors, so she could represent the organization on her own.

"It looks as though everyone's here," the receptionist said. "If you'll just follow me, please, we'll go upstairs to Mrs. Patton's office." Marcie and I hung back, allowing the family to go up the stairs ahead of us before bringing up the rear.

Upstairs, the receptionist ushered us into a large office with a huge bay window overlooking the street below. We saw a middle-aged woman with close-cropped salt-and-pepper hair dressed in a pink tweed suit sitting behind an antique mahogany desk. She rose as we entered and introduced herself as Mrs. Patton, but

she didn't come around the desk or offer to shake hands
with anybody. Seven straight, high-backed, wooden
chairs were arranged in a shallow semi-circle in front of
Mrs. Patton's desk. I took one of the end seats. I already
felt I didn't belong here, and Jennifer's attitude earlier
had put me a bit off-balance as well.

"Would anyone like a drink before we begin?" Mrs.
Patton asked. "Brittany already has both coffee and tea
brewed."

Nancy asked for coffee, and Bunny requested orange
juice.

"Orange juice," Brittany repeated. "I don't believe
we have any. May I bring you something else?"
Brittany asked Bunny.

"Okay. I'll have cranberry juice instead."

"I'm afraid we don't have cranberry juice, either,"
Brittany informed Bunny, whose lips curled in a pout.

"Miss Bourbon, this is a law office, not a
restaurant," Nancy said impatiently. "The choices are
coffee or tea."

A lone tear dribbled down Bunny's face. Justin
pulled his chair closer to her and took her hand.

"Now, Gram. Don't be so hard on Bunny. She didn't
mean anything by it."

"You're right, Justin," Nancy agreed. "I guess we're
all a little tense. I'm sorry, Bunny."

Bunny sniffed and wiped the tear away with the back
of her hand while Justin mouthed "coffee" to Brittany.
We sat in silence for a few minutes, waiting for Brittany
to return with the drinks while Mrs. Patton shuffled
some papers on her desk and fiddled with her computer.

By the time Brittany returned with two cups of
coffee, we were all on edge. Our uncomfortable chairs
didn't help matters much.

"All right. We'll get started," Mrs. Patton said.
"We're here at Matthew Daniels' request. He specified

that, in the event of his untimely death following his knee surgery, we have a formal reading of his will. Let me explain that I won't actually read the will word for word, but I'll summarize the major points pertinent to each of the beneficiaries, who will be provided with the full text of the will at the end of our meeting. When Mr. Daniels signed his will the day before his surgery, he did not expect this meeting to take place. His main objective in making this new will was to have his wishes honored in case the surgery went wrong; however, I can assure you that he was in good spirits and had every confidence that his surgery and recovery would go well. Unfortunately, unforeseen circumstances intervened."

"There's a new will?" Jennifer asked. "Matt made a will right after Justin was born twenty years ago. He never mentioned changing it."

Nancy squeezed Jennifer's hand. "I'm sure there's nothing to worry about, dear."

"Your mother's correct, Mrs. Daniels. You're the primary beneficiary of your husband's estate."

"That can't be right. Matt and I agreed that Justin should be Matt's heir."

"What?" Nancy looked shocked. "You never told me that. What about you?"

"Oh, I was to be provided for, of course, but Matt wanted all the stock he owned in his business to go to Justin. He expected Justin to take over the company one day."

"Dad's always said the company would be mine some day." Justin looked stunned. "That's why I've worked there every summer for the last four years. That's why I'm majoring in business."

Mrs. Patton sighed audibly. "Mr. Daniels didn't share his reasons with me, but he left a confidential sealed letter for each of you, which may provide some insight into his thinking. Let's proceed, shall we?" Mrs. Patton paused briefly. "Mrs. Daniels, as I said, you're the primary beneficiary of your husband's estate. The major assets are his controlling shares of stock in Daniels Insurance Company, Incorporated; real estate, including your residence, your summer home in Minnesota, commercial property in Central City and Des Moines; his portfolio of common stock in a variety of other companies; and a partnership interest in Iowa Insurance Plans, a company specializing in medical insurance for small business owners. In addition, there are numerous certificates of deposit as well as checking and savings accounts at the First Bank of Iowa. I can't tell you what the precise value of the estate is due to the fluctuations in stock prices and the real estate market, but my conservative estimate is that it's somewhere in the neighborhood of sixty million dollars."

"Oh, my word!" Jennifer looked stunned. "I had no idea."

Nancy looked just as shocked as her daughter, and Justin simply looked bewildered.

"But that's not fair!" Bunny protested. We all turned to look at her. "I mean it's not fair to Justin!"

"Shhh. It's okay, Bunny. It's what my father wanted."

"Let's continue. Justin, you'll inherit ten million dollars." A little whoop of joy from Bunny interrupted Mrs. Patton. "If I may continue," she said, staring at Bunny, "to be held in trust until your thirtieth birthday."

"No way!" Bunny said.

"Miss Bourbon, if you can't contain yourself, it might be a good idea if you'd wait for us downstairs," Nancy said.

"I'm afraid that won't do," Mrs. Patton said. "Miss Bourbon is named in Mr. Daniels' will. She should remain here."

Nancy and Bunny began to argue while Jennifer and Justin sought to calm them down. Marcie moved her chair back a few inches and stared down at her hands while Katie didn't try to disguise her interest as she listened to the argument. During the commotion, my phone rang. I had adjusted the volume to its maximum earlier because I didn't want to miss Wes's call."

"Excuse me. This is an emergency call—a sick relative," I said and fled from the room, closing the door behind me. I leaned against the wall in the hallway and silently said a prayer as I answered my phone.

"He's going to be all right!"

"Wes, that's wonderful news!"

"We're all relieved. Dad's always been so healthy. I'm afraid he's going to have to change his diet, and he won't like that much, but his prognosis is excellent, according to the doctors."

"Tell him I'm happy he's on the mend."

"I will. Right now, I'm on the way down to the cafeteria to get some lunch. I hear the food's terrible there, but I haven't eaten all day, and I'm starving. What are you doing?"

"I'm in the middle of that meeting I told you about. I'm not sure how much longer it will last."

"Oh, right. I forgot about that."

"It's no wonder. I'd like to forget about it, too. I'll give you the lowdown later. Right now, you have more important things on your mind. Take care of yourself, and try to get some rest. I love you."

"Love you, too."

I opened the door to Mrs. Patton's office and cautiously peeked in. The argument continued in full swing as I slipped back into my seat and put my phone away in my handbag. I doubted that they'd even noticed I'd left the room for a few minutes. Marcie and I looked at each other and shook our heads. Finally, Mrs. Patton had had enough.

"Please, please, let's settle down. You'll have plenty of time to discuss the terms of the will later." I half expected her to bring out a gavel and start pounding away. She raised her voice slightly. "I'm going to continue. There's more I need to address." She took a deep breath and looked at the family and Bunny sternly.

"C'mon, Bunny. Quiet down," Justin urged. "I want to hear what she has to say."

"Now, then. Justin, as I said, your father has set up a trust for you. Under the terms of Mr. Daniels' will, the trust will be dissolved in your favor on your thirtieth birthday, and you'll gain full control of the funds therein with one proviso. You must not be married to Miss Bourbon at that time and you must not have married her at any time prior to your thirtieth birthday, even if said marriage ends in annulment or divorce. If so, you forfeit all funds in the trust."

"Bunny's my fiancée! How could Dad be so cruel?"

"What are you saying?" Bunny demanded, pointing to Mrs. Patton. "You mean we can't get married?"

"No, Miss Bourbon. That isn't what I'm saying. You and Justin are free to marry, but such a decision will ultimately cost him his inheritance, based on the terms of Mr. Daniels' will."

Bunny's face contorted with anger while Justin hung his head. He appeared to be more resigned than angry. "Don't worry, Bunny. I won't let this stop our marriage. We don't need ten million dollars to be happy."

"It would help," she said sharply.

"We'll talk about this later," Justin assured her. He took her hand, raised it to his lips, and kissed it gently.

"You're always such a gentleman, honey," Bunny said, reverting to her coquettish manner.

Mrs. Patton patted her brow with a tissue. I suppose it was no fun being the bearer of bad news. She had known before the meeting started that some of the beneficiaries weren't going to leave happy, and I imagined that perhaps she had dreaded the prospect of conveying Matt's wishes. No wonder she hadn't interacted with the family while we waited for the meeting to start. Her job was probably easier if she didn't form any bond with the beneficiaries.

"Next. Miss Bourbon, there's a bequest for you."

Bunny leaned forward expectantly.

"You're to receive the sum of one million dollars . . ." Bunny squealed with delight. "I haven't finished," Mrs. Patton informed Bunny. "You're to receive the sum of one million dollars," she repeated, "on the conditions that you never marry Justin Daniels, that you leave the state of Iowa, and that you sign a contract agreeing to those terms."

"He's trying to bribe you, Bunny. My father's dead, but he's trying to buy you off. Don't fall for it," Justin said. "We can do just fine on our own. We don't need his money."

"You're right, honey. He can't control us," she assured Justin, but I could tell the wheels were turning, despite her declaration.

"Katie Reston." Mrs. Patton looked around, and I realized that we'd never introduced ourselves, and she'd never asked us our names.

"Here." Katie held up her hand.

"Ah, yes. Mr. Daniels has left you a sum of one thousand dollars."

"That's all? Only a thousand? I've worked for him for twenty years. Unbelievable!" She sneered, and I fully expected her to make a rude gesture next, but she restrained herself.

"Don't worry, Katie. I'll make it up to you," Jennifer said.

"That's so typical of him," Katie said, sitting up

straighter. "Matt never showed me any respect in twenty years. Why should I expect anything different now that he's gone?"

"I'm sorry, Katie."

"You don't need to be sorry. He didn't respect you, either." She shook her head.

"Maybe you'd better keep your opinions to yourself," Nancy told her.

"It's okay, Mom," Jennifer said, although her expression belied her words. "Please, Mrs. Patton, go on." For a woman who'd just found out that she was a millionaire sixty times over, Jennifer didn't seem very happy. I speculated that she wasn't looking forward to listening to Justin's and Katie's woes when they all returned home after the meeting.

"Yes. The next bequest is of a charitable nature. As the representative of Food for Families, Marcie Nolan . . . ." Mrs. Patton paused and looked from me to Marcie, who held up her hand. "Ah, yes. Marcie Nolan has been asked to attend this meeting. Mr. Daniels has bequeathed five million dollars to Food for Families."

Marcie gasped. "Oh, how generous!" she gushed. "That's wonderful!"

"However, there is one proviso."

Uh, oh, I thought. Now what?

"It's just routine business practice. Mr. Daniels wanted to be sure everything is in order at Food for Families, so he made the donation contingent on an in-depth audit of FFF's finances. When the auditors report that the organization is on sound financial footing, the money will be deposited in FFF's bank account."

"I'll get the audit set up immediately," Marcie said.

Mrs. Patton held up her hand. "Not so fast. There are certain specifications for the audit. That's where you come in, Ms. McMillan."

"Me? But I'm not an auditor. Accounting isn't

exactly my strong suit."

"You don't need to be an accountant to fulfill the terms of Mr. Daniels' bequest to Food for Families. The gist of his bequest to you is that he's left you ten thousand dollars on the condition that you hire an independent auditor to perform an in-depth audit, which must be completed within a week from today."

"I'm still a bit confused that he should want me to do it. Wouldn't something like an audit fall under Marcie's purview as president of the board of directors? I'm not even the treasurer."

"There are other details, which this letter will explain," she said, handing me a white, legal-size envelope.

"Laurel, I'd be happy to help you with the arrangements," Marcie offered.

"Thank you, Marcie."

"I advise you to read the letter before you make any arrangements, Ms. McMillan. You must follow Mr. Daniels' instructions. Should you decide that you'd prefer not to handle this matter, let me know by the end of business today, so that I can make alternate arrangements."

"All right."

"If I don't hear from you, I'll assume that you accept the terms and will perform your duties."

"That's fine. I don't know what to think about all this right now. I'll study the instructions and let you know my decision."

"Yes, please do that, and let me know if there's anything I can help clarify."

I nodded, folded the envelope, and tucked it into my handbag.

"Our business is now concluded," Mrs. Patton said formally as she handed similar envelopes to Jennifer, Justin, and Marcie. "Mrs. Reston, Mr. Daniels didn't leave an envelope for you."

"Whatever," Katie muttered to nobody in particular.

"Brittany will provide each of you a copy of the will downstairs," she said, and we all stood and filed out of Mrs. Patton's office, down the stairs, and into the reception area where Brittany was waiting with a stack of envelopes. She handed each of us an envelope as we reached the bottom of the steps. Still muttering, Katie followed the family out of the back entrance, leaving Marcie and me inside. After asking Brittany the location of the restroom, Marcie disappeared around the corner. I sat down on one of the plush sofas, took the envelope out of my purse, tore open the end, and took out Matt's letter. Glancing at it, I could see that it was formatted like a business memo, but before I started to read the memo, Marcie reappeared.

"Have you read Matt's letter yet?" she asked breathlessly. Before I could answer, she said, "May I see it? I'd be happy to help expedite the audit. It was so generous of Matt to leave Food for Families such a huge donation," she gushed.

Eager as I was to read Matt's letter, I didn't intend to do it with Marcie looking over my shoulder. On the other hand, I didn't want to antagonize her. After all, she'd done a fabulous job in fund raising for FFF, and she was not only a fellow resident of Hawkeye Haven, but also a member of our book club. Since we were both on the board of FFF, I'd be seeing her once a month at our board meetings, too.

"Thanks so much, Marcie," I said as I stuffed the memo back inside its envelope and tucked it inside my purse. "I've been thinking about this, and I admit I'm a little out of my depth here, so I've decided to consult with my own attorney before I do anything. It's possible he may advise me not to proceed."

"Oh, but, Laurel, wouldn't ten thousand dollars be a

nice addition to your checking account?" she said enthusiastically.

"It would, but I doubt that I'd feel right about accepting it. I could donate it to FFF, although that would be just a drop in the bucket compared to Matt's five-million-dollar donation. Also, I bet there must be some ins and outs as far as the tax consequences and so on, so I think seeking counsel is the way to go."

"Another donation! What a super idea! I hope your lawyer doesn't talk you out of it because you know how strapped for funds we always are. Be sure to call me and let me know how I can help."

"Thanks, Marcie," I said, avoiding any commitment. "I should get going now."

We went our separate ways since Marcie hadn't parked in the lot behind the building. The idea of consulting my own lawyer about this whole business had popped into my head while I was talking to Marcie, but I thought now that it wouldn't be a bad idea. I'd babbled about tax consequences just to steer Marcie away from trying to take over the audit, but weren't there always tax consequences? That was one reason that, when I'd first engaged a lawyer in Center City, I'd found one with a dual law and accounting practice, specializing in clients with their own small businesses. I shuddered to think about the student loans Dillon McKenzie, my lawyer, must have had to take out to spend all those years in graduate school. His practice seemed to be thriving, so it must have been worth it, I mused.

As I left, I dug in my purse for my car keys, and I didn't see Justin and Bunny at first, but I heard their raised voices. They were standing next to a red Corvette, which I assumed must belong to Justin.

"I can't help it, Bunny. I didn't even know dad made a new will. He never said anything about it to me or mom."

"He never liked me. Why didn't he like me?" Bunny asked.

"You know why. He kept saying that you're a stripper and that I should marry somebody like mom."

"I'm not a stripper. I'm an exotic dancer! Anyway, I'm a student, too. Doesn't that count for anything?"

"Of course it does! I love you, and we're going to get married. We don't need dad's money. Plenty of people have started out with nothing."

"But it's so *unfair*! You should be able to marry me and inherit his money, too. I don't know why he left almost everything to your mom. You need it more than she does. You have your whole life ahead of you, and she's *old*."

"Hang on there, Bunny. Mom's forty-five. She's not *that* old."

Bunny sniffed and tossed her head. "Maybe you should contest the will."

"That's probably not going to work."

"How do you know? You could try, couldn't you?"

"Bunny, dad made his decision, and I'm not inclined to go against his wishes."

"Well, I suppose I could always take him up on his million-dollar offer and leave town," Bunny flared. "What do you think of that?"

"Calm down, now. You're not serious, are you? I thought you loved me!"

"I do love you, but if you loved me, you'd do something about this stupid will," she yelled.

I'd stopped when I first heard Justin and Bunny arguing because I'd have to walk right past them to get to my car, so I just stood there staring, but they didn't notice me, anyway. I saw that Jennifer's silver BMW was still parked next to Justin's Corvette. Jennifer hadn't started the BMW yet, and I could see Nancy in the front passenger seat and Katie in the back. When Bunny threatened to leave Justin, Jennifer stepped out of her car and approached the couple. I was surprised to see her put her arm around Bunny.

"Please calm down, Bunny. This isn't doing anybody any good. Don't make any decisions until you've had time to reflect on what you want."

"I know what I want. I want to marry Justin, and I want him to contest the will," Bunny said.

"Well, certainly that's an option, but I suspect that Matt's lawyer dotted all the i's and crossed all the t's. Contesting the will could turn out to be a very expensive, uphill battle, but, of course, that's Justin's decision." She looked at Justin. "I'll support you in whatever you decide, but I'm not going to finance a lawsuit."

"I'm not the one who wants to sue, Mom," Justin said plaintively. "Come on, Bunny. Let's go get some lunch. We can talk about it later, okay, babe?"

"So I'm still your 'babe'?"

"You bet."

"Then you should want to keep me happy." She hung her head for a moment.

"Bunny?" Justin cajoled.

"Oh, all right," she agreed. "Kiss, kiss," she said, puckering her lips, but before Justin could move in, she noticed me staring at them.

"What are *you* looking at?" she demanded.

Chapter 12

Feeling as though I qualified for *persona non grata* of the day, I replied, "I'm just going to my car, if you don't mind. It's a little difficult to get there when you're standing right in the middle of the parking lot."

"Whatever," she said, flouncing around the Corvette and plopping in the passenger seat. Justin looked relieved as he closed the door for her. He revved the engine, maneuvered the car around Jennifer and me, and took off, the red sportscar's tires screeching as he rounded the corner into the lane.

"Sorry, Laurel," Jennifer said.

"No need for you to apologize for Bunny's behavior. I know it's a difficult time for everybody. She's had a shock."

"She's not the only one. I didn't have a clue that Matt had amassed a fortune. We always lived well, but not extravagantly." I wasn't sure what Jennifer considered extravagant, considering that last month she'd told me that Matt had given Justin a new Corvette for his twentieth birthday.

"Matt took care of all the finances. I don't know how I'll manage."

"Jennifer, darling, could we leave now?" Nancy called. "It's a bit cool sitting here in the car."

"Of course, Mom. I'll be right there." Jennifer turned to me. "Laurel, I'll let you know about the funeral as soon as we finalize the arrangements. The medical examiner hasn't released Matt's body yet, but Dad's checking with them now, and we're going to the funeral home later this afternoon."

I squeezed Jennifer's arm. "Please let me know if there's anything I can do to help. I do know something of what you're going through."

"Yes, I know. Sometimes I forget you're a widow."

We had widowhood in common, but I thought about how different our circumstances were otherwise as I got into my car and put the key into the ignition. It had been several years since I'd lost my own husband in an auto accident, but Jennifer had just lost Matt only a few days ago, and his death had been no accident. My husband Tim and I didn't have any children, but Jennifer had Justin. Tim and I hadn't accumulated much money, but Jennifer had inherited a large estate. We'd had a good marriage, but I doubted that Jennifer could say the same about hers.

Noticing that I had half an hour before meeting Amy and Cynthia for lunch, I drove around downtown, looking for a parking spot near the Sutton Place boutique hotel, where we planned to lunch. I couldn't park in the hotel lot because it was reserved for hotel guests. After several minutes of cruising around, I was almost tempted to return to Anderson and Patton's parking lot, but if I did that, I'd have to walk back ten blocks, and I'd be late. I tried to remember the name of the side street where Cynthia had planned to park, but I couldn't think of it. Finally, I lucked out when a van backed out of a spot just around the corner from the hotel. Much as I liked the old downtown area of Center City, the lack of parking there factored into my doing most of my shopping at one of the city's malls that were clustered along the highway leading to Interstate 80.

I went into the hotel lobby and glanced around for the restaurant, but I didn't see it, so I stopped at the registration desk to inquire. The clerk pointed upwards, toward a balcony behind me.

"It's on the mezzanine. I'm sorry we don't have our signs installed yet. You can take the elevator or the stairs right around the corner."

At the top of the stairs, the hostess greeted me and asked whether I had a reservation.

"Yes. Laurel McMillan, for three." I scanned the restaurant, but I didn't see Amy and Cynthia. "It looks as though my friends aren't here yet."

"Let me seat you, and I'll bring them to your table as soon as they come in." She led me to a table next to the fireplace. It was a warm and cozy spot. "Coffee?"

"Yes, please." I sat back while she signaled a server who hurried over to fill my cup.

"Would you like to look at the menu while you're waiting?" the hostess asked.

"No, thanks. I'll just wait until they get here. It shouldn't be long."

My phone bleeped, signaling a text message from Cynthia. She hadn't been able to park on the side street as she'd planned, and they'd had to park several blocks away. I texted her back "no worries." The restaurant wasn't busy, and it shouldn't take them more than fifteen minutes to walk over, anyway.

I opened my handbag and pulled out the memo from Matt.

> To: Laurel McMillan, Food for Families Board Director
>
> From: Matthew Daniels, Vice-President, Food for Families Board
>
> Subject: In-Depth Audit of Food for Families
>
> It has come to my attention today that the finances of Food for Families may not be in order. Unfortunately, our treasurer holds his title in name only. He has no background in accounting and leaves it to

the organization's administration to monitor the books. I received an anonymous tip that a substantial amount of money is missing. Because of my impending surgery, I don't have time to follow up on this allegation. I'm asking you to order and oversee a full, in-depth audit, because you seem to be the most sensible and conscientious person on the board, and I believe I can rely on your discretion not to involve Food for Family's president until after you've had a full report from the auditors. I've made my donation of five million dollars to FFF contingent on a satisfactory outcome: either a report from the auditor that FFF's finances are in order or, if not, a solid plan to rectify the situation. I'll leave that to your discretion, as long as the organization is restored to a sound financial basis if any problems are uncovered by the auditor. I've provided for payment to the auditor; all bills should be submitted to Mrs. Patton at Anderson and Patton. I recommend one of the following firms to perform the audit:

There followed a list of four names, one of which happened to be that of my own lawyer, Dillon McKenzie. I didn't like to talk on my phone in a restaurant, but I made an exception in this case. Since nobody was sitting nearby, I made a quick call to Dillon's office, asking for a meeting as soon as possible to discuss an urgent, time-sensitive matter. His receptionist informed me that he could see me at three o'clock, and I breathed a sigh of relief. Surely Dillon could walk me through whatever needed to be done; in fact, I was hoping he'd be able to do the in-depth audit himself, although I realized that his busy schedule might prevent him from accepting the job.

The suggestion that Food for Families was missing money troubled me. How reliable could an anonymous tip be? Perhaps, someone with a grudge was trying to cause problems. On the other hand, if the allegation turned out to be true, I'd be even more dismayed. The administration team at Food for Families consisted of only six people, so if someone was embezzling money from FFF's coffers, it had to be one of them. The only board member who had direct responsibility for money matters was the treasurer, and, as Matt had said, he trusted the office employees to take care of the books, signing off on whatever they gave him without asking any questions about expenditures. I hoped that our treasurer's trust wasn't misplaced.

As I put the letter and my phone back into my handbag, my friends arrived, out of breath from their unexpected downtown hike.

"Sorry we're late, Laurel," Cynthia said. "This is the first time ever I haven't been able to park on Keokuk Street. You know, for a while a few years ago, the downtown area was practically deserted, but now it's busier than ever. I suppose we have the mayor and town council to thank for the revitalization. They really pushed for it."

"I like the old downtown," Amy said, "but there needs to be better parking. I think they should put in a couple of parking lots."

"Amen to that," I agreed. "I got lucky and found a place right around the corner, but I drove around for several minutes before finding it."

Our server appeared, recited the list of daily specials, handed us menus, and took our drink orders. When she returned with our drinks, she also brought a basket of warm muffins, which we wasted no time in sampling.

"Mmm. These are scrumptious," Amy said, popping a bite into her mouth. "I skipped breakfast this morning, so I'll do a twofer for lunch."

Cynthia and I laughed at that as Amy buttered another muffin. At just five feet tall, Amy was not only short, but she was also slender.

"How do you do it, Amy? You never seem to gain an ounce," Cynthia said. "I wish I could say the same."

"I don't know, really. I've never dieted in my life. Exercise maybe? I play a lot of tennis and golf, and now I'm going to dance quite a bit, too."

Just as I was about to ask Amy what she meant about dancing, the server came over to our table to take our orders. Although she eyed the tempting menu longingly, Cynthia settled for a salad. Amy ordered chicken marsala, and I ordered chicken piccata. Since I wasn't much of a cook, I loved to eat out.

As soon as our server left with our orders, I asked Amy, "What was that you were saying about more dancing, Amy?"

"Bud and I have partnered for the next dance competition at the Stars Dance Studio. We're entered to compete in cha-cha, tango, and foxtrot."

"That makes me tired just hearing about it," Cynthia said. "I'll stick to golf myself. The last time Pete and I danced was at our thirtieth anniversary party four years ago, and we stepped all over each other's toes."

"I'm impressed, too, Amy," I said. "Wes and I stick strictly to the slow dances, and even then, it's all we can do to avoid bumping into another couple."

"When's the competition, Amy?" Cynthia asked. "I'd really like to see you in action."

"It's in six weeks. I can't remember the exact date, but I'll look it up, and let you know."

"I'd love to come," I said.

"Great! It's always nice to have some fans in the

audience. We just started rehearsing last week, and we have a long way to go. We're practicing every day for several hours."

"How exhausting!" Cynthia exclaimed.

"I'm a bit surprised Bud can keep up that pace," I said.

"I know. You'd never guess it by looking at him, but Bud's doing fine at rehearsals."

"Maybe I shouldn't ask, but is Bud becoming more than your dance partner?" Curiosity often led me into trouble, but I didn't really think Amy would mind my asking. She was always the first to find out about any new romances in Hawkeye Haven, and she loved playing matchmaker, too. Her coffee table was always loaded with stacks of romance novels.

"Well, you're not the first one to ask me that, but the answer's no. We're just friends. Before FFF's fund raiser, I knew him only through your Perfect Pillows class, but when we started dancing, we really hit it off."

"I'm glad to hear that," Cynthia said, "because he's old enough to be your father."

"Now, mother hen, don't worry about me. I arranged for Bud to meet Sandy, my librarian friend, who's about his age. They've already gone out on three dates!"

"Oh, good," I said. I knew Sandy, too. "I think you've made another match."

"I hope so. Bud's been very lonely since his wife died, and he needs a woman in his life. I'm just not ready to date again. It's only been a year since Jim died, and most of the time, I can only make it through the day by constantly keeping busy. I miss him so much. I blame Matt Daniels, but now he's gone, too. If it weren't for him, I'd still be a married woman."

"I'm confused," I said. "What did Matt have to do with Jim's death? I thought he had a heart attack."

"Yes, but it was brought on by stress," Amy said.

"You were in Seattle at the time visiting your parents, I think," Cynthia added.

I nodded. "That's right. I remember how shocked I was when I heard the news." My condolence call to Amy had been long distance, and we'd spent all our time on the phone weeping. By the time I returned home from Seattle, Amy had gone to stay with her daughter in the East, and she hadn't returned to Hawkeye Haven until about six months ago. Although she often mentioned Jim and how much she missed him, this was the first time I'd heard that she held Matt Daniels responsible for his death.

"Jim was so happy when Iowa Insurance Plans hired him as sales director, but it turned out to be a nightmare. Matt was one of three partners, but the other two must have been silent partners because they were never involved in the day-to-day company business. Sales spiked a lot after Jim started working there, but it was never enough for Matt. He was continually on Jim's back. Every day at work was like living in a pressure cooker for Jim. Matt used to call meetings at the drop of a hat, often in the middle of the night or on weekends. One Saturday, we had planned to take a nice drive in the country, stop for lunch, and then do some antiquing in the afternoon, but Matt called at four o'clock that morning, raging about one of the sales staff, and he demanded that Jim come into the office to talk about it. I suggested that he skip the meeting and resign. He said that he had been thinking about resigning, but he wanted to find another job first. When I kissed him good-bye, I didn't know it would be the last time. He had a heart attack during the meeting, and he was gone before the ambulance arrived." Tears rolled down Amy's face, as Cynthia put her arm around her and I reached for Amy's hand.

"How awful!" I hadn't realized Jim worked for Matt,

but when Amy mentioned Iowa Insurance Plans, I remembered that Jennifer had inherited Matt's partnership interest in the firm. "Matt sounds like a terrible boss."

"The worst," Amy agreed. "People tell me I shouldn't blame him, that Jim could have had a heart attack, anyway, but I'm not so sure about that. I truly believe Jim would still be alive if he'd never worked for Matt."

"So that's why you always stay on the other side of the room from Matt when we have FFF board meetings. I kind of wondered."

"Yes. It's all I could do to be civil to the man. Sitting at the same table with him at the gala was excruciating, but dancing with Bud saved me from having to be there most of the evening."

"Ladies, here we are," our server interrupted, setting our plates in front of us. After we thanked her and assured her that we didn't need anything else at the moment, we sampled our dishes and began eating. Our conversation turned to the food, and then Cynthia diplomatically guided it to lighter topics. When she suggested that we all check out the new boutique next door to the hotel after lunch, Amy and I agreed enthusiastically.

I was grateful to Cynthia for gently steering Amy away from thoughts of her husband's death, but I couldn't help thinking that Amy had a motive for wanting Matt dead, and Amy had been one of the book club members who visited the powder room during our meeting Sunday afternoon. Only a few more steps into the back hallway would have taken her to the bedroom where Matt was recuperating. All possible, but sheer speculation. Amy is one of the sweetest people I know; I simply couldn't picture her smothering a man to death, even if she despised him, and I put the thought out of my head.

After deciding to forgo dessert, although the lemon meringue pie on the dessert cart the server wheeled to our table looked especially tempting to me, we settled our bill, agreeing that we'd come back again soon.

"I do hope they make a go of this place," Cynthia whispered as we were leaving. "It certainly wasn't very busy in here today."

"So do I. I really liked the chicken marsala, and the bite I had of your chicken piccata was wonderful, too," Amy said.

"Maybe business will pick up. It may take a while for the word to get out," I said. We walked down the wide staircase, and the woman at the check-in desk thanked us for coming, asking us to tell our friends about the restaurant.

"We certainly will," Cynthia said. "It was great!"

Once we were outside on the sidewalk, Cynthia said, "It's just as I thought: they're not attracting the locals, and I think the lack of parking has a lot to do with it. I'm going write a letter to the city council and call the mayor."

"You ought to run for mayor, Cynthia," I suggested.

"Oh, no, don't be silly. You can't be serious," she said.

"I *am* serious. I don't know anybody who has more initiative than you, and you're always very efficient, organized, and on top of everything," I said, warming even more to the idea, although it had just popped in my head when Cynthia mentioned writing a letter to the city council.

"Laurel's right. I think it's a super idea."

"Oh, you girls can't be serious. Whatever would Pete think?"

"I bet he'd volunteer to be your campaign manager," I said. I could easily picture Cynthia's husband in that role.

"Hmm. I don't know about that," Cynthia demurred, but she didn't say no.

"Here we are," Amy said, looking at a powder blue tunic displayed with other blue and white clothing in the window of Veronique's Boutique. We entered the shop and found it bigger than it had first appeared from the narrow storefront because the space extended back quite a ways.

"Good afternoon, and welcome to Veronique's," said a tall fifty-something woman with curly chestnut hair. "Please let me know if I can help you find something or you have any questions."

"Are you Veronique, by any chance?" Cynthia asked.

"Well, yes and no. My name's actually Vera, but Veronique sounded more boutique-y to me when I chose a name."

"You have a beautiful shop," Amy said.

"Thank you. Please feel free to browse and try on anything you like. Dressing rooms are in the back."

We wandered around the shop, stopping frequently to admire its unique clothing and jewelry on display. By the time we'd reached the glass jewelry counter next to the check-out area in the middle of the store, I was feeling quite warm in my brown wool cape, so I slipped it off to carry over my arm.

When Vera saw Amy looking at a pair of glitzy rhinestone earrings, she moved behind the counter and asked Amy whether she'd like to try them on. Amy said that she would. Vera turned the mirror on the top of the counter toward Amy and encouraged her to take a look.

"These would add some nice sparkle to my dance costumes," she said, turning toward Cynthia and me. "What do you think?"

We both agreed, and Amy asked Vera to hold them

for her until she finished shopping.

I was leaning over the counter to look at an intricately beaded bracelet when Vera complimented me on my necklace and earrings.

"Thanks, Vera. I made them myself," I said.

"Really? You don't happen to sell any of your jewelry wholesale, do you? I like to keep my inventory unique, and I prefer to buy things from local designers."

"Well, as a matter of fact, I do. It's not my main business, but some of my jewelry is in a few boutiques in Des Moines and Seattle." I continued in my sales mode. "I have some other examples I can show you." I pulled my phone out of my bag and showed her several pictures of jewelry I'd made.

"Do you offer terms or consignment?" Vera asked.

"No, I'm sorry. I don't do enough wholesale business to be able to extend credit, and I've had a few bad experiences with consignments in the past. I'm afraid it's half payment on order and half due on delivery. I could deliver it to you myself. That would save the delivery charge." I didn't blame Vera for asking. I knew how tough it was for a boutique owner to stay in the black, but experience had taught me that I had to look out for my own interests. If I didn't get paid, I would be wasting my time and losing all the supplies I used to make the jewelry. After extending terms to a boutique that placed a large order and then went out of business and having some jewelry stolen from a store where I had it offered on consignment, I'd learned my lesson.

"All right. I really like your wire-wrapped pendants. Could we start with several of those in different colors and shapes."

"Certainly." As we discussed the details of Vera's order and the various stones she preferred, Cynthia and Amy wandered around the store, each selecting a few garments to try on. I caught up with them in the back, as I tucked Vera's check for two hundred dollars into my purse. Although I was happy to have the order, it seemed paltry compared to the ten thousand dollars Matt had left me to oversee the audit, but I was still determined to donate his money to FFF.

"Looks like you made a sale," Cynthia said. "Congrats!"

"Thanks. Who knew I'd actually make money from a shopping trip instead of spending it?" We all laughed.

"I'm going to try on these tops," Amy said.

"I'll wait for you out here, and then I'll try these on," Cynthia said, draping a couple of long cardigans over the back of the sofa that faced the dressing room. "It looks like only one dressing room's free right now."

"Okay. You can give me your opinion," Amy said.

"Oh, Laurel, I meant to tell you to take a look at that rack of caftans over there." Cynthia gestured toward the side wall. "I bet Liz would love those. You might want to tell her about them."

"I'll check it out. In fact, she decided to cut her Florida trip short, and she's coming back this Sunday. Let me take a quick peek."

I was admiring the beading on the brightly colored silk caftans, when I heard a couple of familiar voices, but I couldn't place them right away. I looked over, and I could see their reflections in a mirror that hung at an angle: Nancy and her sister, Jennifer's aunt Barbara. They were busy looking through a packed rack of clothing, and they didn't notice me.

"I just had to take a breather, but I feel guilty leaving Jennifer at home," Nancy said. "I told her to lie down for a few hours before we have to go to the funeral home. It's already been a stressful day what with Justin and Bunny at each other's throats on top of everything else."

"You've been there for her every step of the way. Don't beat yourself up for wanting to get out of the house for a while. We can't be with her every minute. I'm going to have to go back to work next week."

"I know. You've already taken a week off, but Mark and I plan to stay as long as Jennifer needs us. She's feeling very guilty, especially now that she's inherited the bulk of Matt's estate, although I keep reassuring her that she shouldn't. It's not her fault that awful nurse decided to take her revenge on Matt when he couldn't defend himself. If anything, Jennifer should be relieved Edna saved her the trouble of filing for divorce."

Chapter 13

Had Jennifer told her mother she planned to divorce Matt, or was Nancy implying that Jennifer *should have wanted* to divorce Matt? I froze in my tracks and stood perfectly still, until they moved off toward the front of the store, before I backtracked to join Cynthia. Even though I hadn't been deliberately eavesdropping, Nancy and Barb would have assumed that I had if they'd seen me, and I'd had enough of Jennifer's family drama for one day.

Sitting next to Cynthia on the sofa, I watched Amy pirouette as she modeled a bright red top.

"What do you think?" Amy asked. It wasn't a rhetorical question, nor was Amy fishing for compliments. She genuinely wanted our opinions.

"Red's a great color on you, Amy," I said, "but I think the top's too long for you."

"I agree, and it looks a little wide in the shoulders," Cynthia said.

Amy cast a critical look in the mirror and sighed. "You're right. I love the color, but I think I'll pass on this one." While she was in the dressing room, Vera came back to see how we were doing.

"Any luck, ladies?"

"Amy found a top she wants to buy," Cynthia said.

"I'll take this one," Amy said, as she came out of the dressing room and handed Vera a pastel floral top.

"It'll be waiting for you at the register," Vera said. "I'll put the ones you don't want back."

"Thank you." Amy turned to Cynthia. "Your turn."

She whispered to me, "Whoever's in that other dressing room must be buying out the store, or else she's very slow. She hasn't come out since we've been here."

After Cynthia disappeared into the dressing room, we heard voices behind us, and I figured Nancy and Barb were making their way to the dressing rooms. Sure enough, they each held a couple garments draped over their arms. When they saw us, they looked surprised.

"Hello," Barb said. "I know I met both of you the other day, but I'm sorry I can't remember your names. So many people have come by the house."

"I'm Amy, and this is Laurel. Our friend is in the dressing room right now. The other one's occupied, too. Sit here while you're waiting," she said, patting the sofa.

"Nancy, why don't you sit here, next to Barb, and I'll bring that chair over." I quickly got up and re-positioned an armchair at a right angle next to the sofa.

"You girls must think it's terrible for us to be shopping now," Nancy said.

"Not at all. Sometimes, we all need to take a break," Amy said.

Cynthia came out of the dressing room and spoke to Nancy and Barb. "Hello. I'm Cynthia," she said tactfully. I suspected she'd heard Barb's comment and wanted to save her any more embarrassment.

Nancy nodded and said, "I know Jennifer hasn't contacted people yet about Matt's funeral, but we're going to the funeral home to make arrangements this afternoon. It's scheduled for one o'clock Monday afternoon."

We all told Nancy that we'd be there. I suspected Amy would prefer to skip it, but I knew she'd attend to support Jennifer. Realizing that I'd be late for my appointment with Dillon if I didn't leave soon, I said my good-byes, telling Amy I needed to talk to her about some FFF board business and that I'd call her later. I wanted her to hear about Matt's donation and the audit from me, but since Nancy knew about it too, I couldn't be sure that she wouldn't tell Amy first. At least, I'd given Amy a heads-up. When I left, Amy, Barb, and Nancy were complimenting Cynthia on the cardigans she'd tried on.

As soon as I reached my car, I pulled out my phone, intending to text Wes. I saw that he'd already texted me, assuring me that his father's progress continued. He planned to go back to his parents' house for a few hours of sleep and said he'd call me when he woke up later in the evening.

I'd put the phone aside and started the car when my phone peeped, signaling a new email message. I read it as soon as I saw that it originated from FFF. Marcie had sent out an email blast to our supporters, telling them about Matt's large donation. I'd assumed she'd hold off the announcement until after the audit, but we hadn't discussed strategy, and her public relations skills exceeded mine, so I figured she knew what she was doing. It also made me think she had nothing to hide from the auditor. She must have confidence that FFF's finances were in good order.

I made it to Dillon's office just in time for my three o'clock appointment. He was walking out of his private office, talking with another client when I came in the front door.

"'Good timing, Laurel," Dillon said. "I'll be right with you."

I chatted with his receptionist, Kelly, while Dillon finished his conversation with his client. Then we headed into Dillon's office. He'd recently re-decorated it, and I hadn't yet seen the "after" version. The "before" version had been Spartan, to say the least, so I was astonished when I saw an office that looked like it could have been featured in an upscale decorating magazine or television show. The massive oak desk, burnt sienna walls, custom bookshelves filled with law books, hardwood floors, Persian area rug, plush leather furniture, and colorful abstract art on the walls projected just the right ambiance for an up-and-coming attorney's office. I guessed a hike in Dillon's fees would be coming soon.

"Beautiful office, Dillon," I said.

"Isn't it great?" he enthused. "Look at this," he said, as a panel on his desk slid aside and a computer rose from its depths. "Awesome, huh?"

I smiled. He sounded like a kid with a new toy. "Totally awesome! How does it work?"

"Just press a button under here," he said, indicating the desk top. "And voilà." The computer sank back into the recesses of the desk as he pushed the button. "Now, what can I help you with? Kelly said you have an urgent matter to discuss." He grabbed a pen and a yellow legal pad. His preference for low-tech methods reminded me of Wes, who always had a notebook and pencil at hand. Even so, I knew both Wes and Dillon logged plenty of computer time.

I quickly explained Matt's bequest and the part he'd asked me to play in overseeing an in-depth audit of Food for Families before handing him Matt's letter and my copy of Matt's will.

"What do you think, Dillon? Should I oversee the audit or pass? Do you have time to do the audit yourself?"

"I'll make time, if that's what you want. Do I detect a hint of hesitation?"

"Just a smidge. I don't really feel qualified, but since you're willing to do the audit, I'm in. I want to donate the money to FFF, so if you could take care of whatever needs to be done tax-wise, I'd be grateful."

"Sure, that's not a problem. I'll see to it. By the way, I'm raising my hourly fee, but only for new clients. Matt's estate will fall under that category, though."

"I understand. Yours is one of the firms Matt recommended, so that's fine."

"All right, then. Let's get this show on the road. Food for Families must have a procedure set forth in the by-laws for initiating an audit. You don't happen to have a copy of the by-laws with you, do you?"

"No, but board members have access to FFF's documents in the Cloud. Let me look up the log-in. Ah, here it is."

Dillon called up his computer again and found FFF's by-laws. It didn't take him long to discover what he was looking for. "We need to contact FFF's treasurer because he's charged with initiating any audit."

"I don't have his number in my phone, but I can get it," I said, as I called Amy, but my call went straight to voice mail, and I guessed that she'd already gone to the dance studio to rehearse. I shook my head, "No luck."

"What's his name? Maybe he has a publicly listed number."

"Roger Schultz."

"He does," Dillon said, after a few keystrokes. "Before we call him, here's what I have in mind . . ."

Fifteen minutes later, we were waiting for Roger in the parking lot of the strip mall, where FFF's administrative offices were located on the second floor above a pizza parlor. The out-of-the-way spot didn't affect FFF's mission since food donations, distribution, and events all happened in other places. Roger arrived, carefully parking his old Lincoln town car away from the other cars in the lot, and Dillon and I climbed out of our cars to meet him. I introduced the two men, and they shook hands.

"I was so happy when I heard about Matt's huge donation, but hearing from you changed my mood in a big hurry. I surely hope there's no problem with the books," Roger said, running his hand through his mane of white hair. "I admit I leave it to the staff to take care of things."

"We don't know anything yet, Mr. Schultz," Dillon said.

"I understand, but Matt Daniels never acted on a whim in his life, so I'm plenty worried."

"Let's not get ahead of ourselves, Mr. Schultz," Dillon said.

"If Dillon finds a problem, I'm sure he can advise us on a solution so that FFF will be able to get the donation," I assured him.

"I appreciate that, Laurel. I feel bad that I didn't keep a closer eye on things, but that's going to change, I can assure you. I guess we'd better get this over with."

We climbed the stairs and entered FFF's administrative offices, a large space that had a conference room and Marcie's private office partitioned off on the far side. The rest of the employees each had a desk in the larger open area. The stark space contrasted sharply with Dillon's luxurious, re-decorated office.

No receptionist greeted us. FFF didn't employ a receptionist because members of the public seldom visited the offices. Donations came in through the organization's website and various fundraising events in Center City. FFF also received several large grants every year, which helped fill its coffers and justified a full-time grant writer on staff. Matt's donation of five million dollars was the largest single influx of funds FFF had ever had, though. No wonder Marcie couldn't wait to inform our supporters.

As we walked to the back, Roger and I greeted the five staffers who worked at their desks, but we didn't stop to chat. The door to Marcie's small office was open. I knocked lightly on the door frame and asked her to join us in the conference room next door.

The four of us sat at one end of the long conference table. Before I could introduce Marcie to Dillon, Roger spoke up, telling Marcie that he was ordering an audit and that Dillon would be the auditor.

"Of course, Roger. I assume this is due to Matt's bequest."

She looked at me, and I nodded. "We'll have the books ready to look over in about a week," Marcie said agreeably. "Our bookkeeper was out with the flu all last week, and she hasn't caught up yet."

"Not next week. Now," Roger said. "In fact, we need to tell her to stop work immediately, and you can put her on some other tasks while we're taking care of this."

"But what about our disbursements? We have bills to pay."

"That can wait," Dillon interjected. "I'll try to keep the time minimal, but there can't be any payments made until after the audit. I'll need complete access to your computer system and bank accounts. I assume you use physical checks occasionally?"

"We do," Roger said.

"No physical checks should be written during the audit. Roger, can you take charge of those?"

"But that's ridiculous," Marcie sputtered. "Are you saying we can't even write a check for office supplies?"

"As I explained, it's only for a short time. You or staff members can pay for small items out of your own pockets and submit your bills for reimbursement as long as Roger or I have approved the purchase ahead of time."

"This all seems quite extreme," Marcie complained. "Anyway, doesn't our board need to vote to approve an in-depth audit? When I learned about Matt's bequest, I just assumed we'd vote on it at the board meeting next week."

"A board vote isn't necessary, according to FFF's bylaws," Dillon said. "The organization's treasurer may order one at any time."

"And I'm ordering it now," Roger said. "Laurel, Dillon, and I need to stay here for a while to take care of some details, but there's no need for you to stay. We'll keep you posted."

"Okay. Thanks for your help, Roger. I'm sure we all want to get through this as soon as possible so that Matt's donation can be disbursed to FFF. Just think how much good we can do with five million dollars!" I wanted to leave on a positive note, but Marcie looked anything but positive as I walked out of the conference room.

Josh, Marcie's assistant, saw me coming out of the conference room and came over to talk to me.

"Isn't it great?" he asked. "I'm blown away that Mr. Daniels left FFF so much money. I knew that he was putting the donation in his will, but I never expected he'd die so soon."

"I'm sure he didn't expect it, either." I looked at Josh in astonishment. "How in the world did you know about the bequest?" Matt's own wife hadn't known anything about it.

"Oh. He told Marcie about it, and then she told me, but she swore me to secrecy. I didn't think keeping quiet about Mr. Daniels' plans mattered anymore, though, now that the cat's out of the bag. Since FFF will be getting so much money, I don't suppose there's a chance of a small raise for the staffers," he said hopefully.

Chapter 14

"I see," I said, although I didn't understand why Matt would confide his plans in Marcie but not tell Jennifer. I remembered that she'd said Matt handled all their finances, so perhaps it didn't occur to him to inform her. "As for a raise, I can't promise anything, but I'll make sure the subject of employee compensation gets on our agenda at the next regular board meeting." Like most non-profits, Food for Families wasn't able to reward their employees too handsomely for their hard work.

"Thank you so much! I know everybody would appreciate it."

"Let's not get the staffers' hopes up in the meantime," I said. "All I can do is bring up the subject; I can't guarantee results."

Josh nodded, but I feared he heard only what he wanted to hear and that my promise to him would soon be fodder for gossip among the staffers at FFF. I'd successfully avoided becoming embroiled in office politics since I'd gone full-time with my DIY Diva business many years ago, but after college, I'd worked in an office at a large company for a few years, where I'd observed office politics up close. I realized that I probably shouldn't have made the commitment to Josh to put the employee pay raises on the board's agenda, even though I agreed that FFF could justify raises in light of Matt's donation. If the board didn't go along with my suggestion, Josh and the other staffers might just blame me. Another issue that I should have considered involved the chain of command at FFF. Josh's request should have gone to Marcie, not me, and I should have referred him to her when he brought up the subject of employee raises. I decided I should call Marcie later and tell her what I'd said in an attempt to head off a problem. While it hadn't been my intention to cause one, I thought now that, due to my distraction over the audit, maybe I had. No wonder I hated office politics!

I was eager to go home to try to decompress, and nothing helped me do that more than spending time with Bear. When I'd realized that I'd be away from the house much longer than I'd planned, I'd called my neighbor Fran Wells and asked her to check on Bear. Fran and her husband Brian often watched Bear when I was away, and I returned the favor by dogsitting their golden retriever Goldie for them. Luckily, Fran had been home when I called, and she volunteered to pick up Bear so that he and Goldie could have a doggie play date.

When I arrived home, it was well past sunset. After I pulled my car into the garage, I opened the door to the dark hallway and flicked on the light switch before walking across the street to the Wellses' house to pick up Bear. I could hear Bear and Goldie barking before I knocked on the door.

Brian opened the door before I had a chance to knock.

"Come in," he said as both dogs rushed to my side. I stooped and put an arm around each dog, which was a little bit hard to manage since they were both wiggling with joy.

"I hope Bear behaved himself," I said, as Brian and I made our way into the den, where Fran was watching television. Our progress was slowed by both dogs' vying for attention along the way.

"He always does," Brian said.

Fran muted the sound on the show she was watching. "Hi, Laurel. You should have seen Goldie and Bear playing fetch with Brian in the backyard this afternoon. I shot some video of it and posted it on Facebook. They were all out there for a couple of hours, and when they came in, Goldie and Bear were both so exhausted they took a long nap."

"Maybe I should have taken one, too," Brian said, stifling a yawn. "It was such a nice day that it felt good to be outside after the terrible weather we've been having."

"Laurel, take a look at this," Fran said, handing me her phone. "Isn't that the cutest picture?" Fran had taken a photo of Bear and Goldie, fast asleep, cuddled up together on Goldie's bed in the den.

"How adorable! Could you text that picture to me? You always take such great shots."

"Sure. I'll do it right now."

"Thanks, and thank you for taking care of Bear. I guess we'd better be on our way now. Oh, look at that!" Bear trotted to me, his leash dangling from his mouth.

"Well, if that isn't a hint, I never saw one," Fran declared. "I've never seen him do that before."

"Neither have I. Maybe he would have if he could get to his leash, but I always keep it in a drawer at home."

"I usually hang the leashes in the laundry room, but I remember now that I put Bear's on the bar stool after I picked him up."

"Okay, Bear. Mommy can take a hint," I told him as I clipped his leash to his collar. "Thanks, again," I called as we departed.

Since the next item on Bear's agenda was his dinner, he followed me around the house as I turned on lights, hung up my coat, and exchanged my boots for slippers.

I surveyed my nearly barren refrigerator and came away thankful that I'd had a fabulous lunch because I didn't have much on hand for dinner. Finally, I decided on a cheese sandwich with some spicy mustard, but finding I was out of bread, too, I settled on cheese and crackers, resolving to put a trip to the grocery store on my to-do list for tomorrow. I might have been short on food for myself, but I'd never let that happen to Bear, as I maintained a standing order for delivery of his primo dog food. As I dished it out, Bear stood at my side in eager anticipation, and as soon as I put his bowl down, he gobbled it all in less than a minute. Nobody could ever accuse my Lab of being a picky eater.

He must still have been tired from his romp with Goldie and Brian because he headed straight to his bed, flopped down, and fell asleep before I finished eating my cheese and crackers.

Surrounding myself with pillows and pulling a comfy afghan over my lap, I settled down on the sofa in the den to call Tracey so that I could bring her up to speed. Since she hadn't been able to go to the police department with me for fingerprinting the day after Matt's murder, we hadn't seen each other since our disastrous book club meeting. She'd just learned that her boss had scheduled a last-minute consultation with a client in Dallas, so she'd be away for a few days, and she wouldn't be able to attend Matt's funeral. I offered to order flowers from both of us. Although Tracey's job took her out of town fairly often, she thrived on her busy schedule and showed no signs of desiring to slow down.

Next, I put in another call to Amy, although she hadn't responded to my earlier voice mail yet, but she didn't answer. When she'd said she and Bud practiced several hours a day, she hadn't been kidding. I'd hoped that after I gave Amy the scoop about Matt's bequest to

FFF and the in-depth audit, she would contact the other board members since she'd been on FFF's board longer than I had and knew the other board members better than I did. I decided not to wait, though, because I thought the board members should know about the audit before an FFF staffer asked one of them what was going on, so I sent a brief email message to all the board members to let them know about the audit and the reason I was overseeing it. I told them I'd share the results with the board when Dillon had completed his work.

That chore completed, I called Wes, hoping I wouldn't be waking him from a nap, but he picked up right away, and I knew from the chipper way he answered that he'd had some rest.

"How's your dad this evening?"

"It's amazing how much better he looks already. The doctor talked with us a few minutes ago, and he told dad that he'd probably be able to go home in a few days and that he could expect to be back on the golf course in a few weeks."

"That's incredible! He just had heart surgery this morning. I'm really happy. How's your mom doing?"

"Very relieved. We've all had quite a scare, but, now that we know he's going to be all right, we can relax. I'll probably fly back after we get him settled in at home, but Denise's going to stay for a week or two to help out. Dad's not likely to act like an invalid, but he does need to take it easy for a while. Mom and Denise will be better at seeing that he follows doctor's orders than I would be. He's already telling me I should get back to work."

"In that case, he definitely sounds likes he's on the mend. I'm sending him a card tomorrow and a plant to the house, I think, rather than flowers to the hospital."

"Thanks, sweetheart. I know both mom and dad will

appreciate it."

"I'm really sorry I didn't get the card off today, but what a day I've had!" I gave Wes a quick rundown on the day's events.

"Wow! Five million dollars is quite a donation. I can't say I liked Matt, but the money will benefit a lot of people, and so will your donation. I hope the audit doesn't uncover any problems. You said that Matt received an anonymous tip. I can tell you, from my experience with tipsters who won't give the police their names, that most of their tips turn out to be worthless. Some of them like to cause trouble or have an ax to grind, and, unfortunately, some of them do it just to get attention."

"I hope it turns out to be nothing, too. Even if that's the case, one good thing came out of it. Our treasurer's taking his responsibilities very seriously now. I doubt that he'll slack off again after this. Roger's very concerned, and I don't think that he'll ever leave all the financial details entirely to the staff again. If Matt had known that Roger would step up as he has, I'm sure he would have asked him to oversee the audit instead of me. I'm keeping my fingers crossed that nothing's wrong, but I'll be glad when it's over. Numbers and I don't always get along."

"You'll get through it, and so will FFF. From what you've told me, Dillon's something of a bulldog."

"That's true. He won't quit until he gets to the bottom of an issue."

"Leave it in his hands, then. You'll know what's going on soon enough."

"You're right. I resolve to stop thinking about the audit for the rest of the night."

"Good. Actually, I have something to tell you on another subject that might get your mind off it, although I don't know whether that's a good thing or bad in this case."

"What do you mean?"

"Remember when I told you I'd see what I could find out about Edna's son?"

"I sure do. So much has happened since then, I haven't thought about it. What's the story?"

"Edna's son's last name is Fisher, not Elkins. I remember his case, too, although I wasn't the arresting officer."

"He must have done something awful to have a life sentence."

"A judge sentenced him to life in prison after he attacked and killed a guard in the state penitentiary. At the time, Fisher was serving a five-year sentence for burglary and assault with a deadly weapon. He was in his mid-twenties when he was arrested, and it wasn't the first time. He'd been in and out of the county lock-up several times on minor charges. His juvenile record's sealed, but suffice it to say, he had one."

"Sounds as though he was trouble from an early age."

"Yes, and here's the kicker. You wanted to know why Matt and Edna argued. The last stop on Jacob Fisher's burglary spree was the Danielses' house, and Matt was home at the time Fisher broke in. Fisher held Matt at gunpoint, then knocked him out. Even though Fisher wore a mask, Daniels recognized his voice. I think Edna tried to persuade Daniels not to go to the police, but he pressed charges. Fisher wasn't much of a thief because several items from the Danielses' home were found in Fisher's bedroom at his mother's house."

"That's quite a story. I'm surprised I haven't heard anything about it around the community."

"With all the gossip that goes on in Hawkeye Haven, so am I."

"Very funny. I have to admit you're right, though. It

is a bit odd. More to the point, Edna may blame Matt for her son's incarceration, so she had a motive to murder Matt. I know other people were in the house at the time Matt died, and Edna sounds convincing when she denies she smothered Matt, but maybe the right person's in jail."

"Do I detect a shadow of a doubt?"

"Just a smidgen. Oh, I don't know. Edna's the most maddening person ever. She fibs so much that it's hard to discern when she's telling the truth. Anyway, on to a more pleasant topic: I can't wait till you come home. I miss you!" We talked for several more minutes before Wes's mother decided they should all leave the hospital so that his dad could get some sleep.

Since the reading of Matt's will, I'd focused on the audit of FFF, but even though I hadn't actively tried to find out whether anybody except Edna had a reason to want Matt dead, I'd learned that two people who'd been on the scene the day Matt died may have had motives of their own. Amy had spoken bitterly about Matt's actions as Jim's boss, and she blamed Matt for her husband's heart attack. I knew that long-term stress could be dangerous, and I'd heard that stress could trigger a heart attack, but I didn't know whether or not it really was possible. The important thing was that Amy thought that's exactly what happened to Jim. Still, I couldn't picture Amy sneaking into the bedroom, standing over Matt as he slept, poised to kill him, smothering him with Jennifer's prize-winning pillow, and returning to our book group totally unflustered. Few people could pull that off, and I didn't believe Amy was one of them.

On the other hand, Jennifer might be. Most of the time she seemed very controlled. Jennifer reminded me of the iconic Hitchcock cool blonde, but there had been several times since Matt's murder when she expressed emotion, although it faded quickly. She'd seemed upset when we discovered that Matt wasn't breathing, but she'd blamed Matt for insisting on recuperating at home. She'd cried when a crime scene tech confiscated her peacock pillow and bagged it as evidence, and I'd wondered at the time whether she cared more about her beautifully designed and constructed pillow than she did her husband. She'd spoken to me sharply on seeing me waiting at Anderson and Patton this morning, but she quickly backtracked and apologized. Still, all of Jennifer's behavior could be explained by the shock of her husband's unexpected death. If Jennifer had killed Matt, what was her motive? Obviously, the two didn't have the world's best marriage, but why smother Matt if she planned to divorce him anyway? Or did she? Perhaps, divorcing Matt was something her mother thought she should do, not Jennifer's own plan. Then there was the money. Lots and lots of money. Jennifer was a very wealthy woman, thanks to her inheritance from Matt. The desire for money could be the most powerful motivator of all, but Jennifer hadn't known that she was Matt's primary beneficiary, or so she said.

My speculations hadn't led me anywhere except to more doubt, and I resolved not to dwell on thoughts of murder and motives while I was tired. It had been a long day, and I could always focus on a problem better when I felt rested. Just as I was about to rouse Bear from his evening nap to tell him it was time for night-night, my phone chimed. I was happy to see that Amy was calling because she'd been out of touch for hours.

"Hi, Amy. I was starting to wonder if you were going to rehearse all night," I said.

"No, but we did rehearse for a couple of hours. Cynthia dropped me off at the dance studio on her way home, and Bud gave me a ride home after rehearsal, but I forgot to turn my phone back on. A few minutes ago, I suddenly realized I hadn't heard from anyone for quite a while, and that's when I went looking for my cell. I hadn't even taken it out of my handbag when I got home. So, long story short, I just read your email about the audit. Was that the FFF business you mentioned wanting to tell me?"

"Yes, it was. Evidently, shortly before his surgery, Matt had received an anonymous tip that FFF's finances might not be in order. He didn't have time to investigate the allegation himself, but he did have time to make arrangements for it to be investigated in case he didn't survive the surgery. I think he planned to look into any possible irregularities himself as soon as he could after the surgery, but, of course, he never got the chance."

"Well, you know I didn't care for the man myself, and that's an understatement, but I have to say he always took his duties as a board member seriously and always made a large donation whenever we held a fundraiser. I'm astounded that he left FFF so much money, though. I wonder what his family thinks about that."

"They didn't seem to have a problem with it. In fact, Jennifer's inherited far more than the five million FFF will be receiving, and Justin stands to inherit, too, as long as he doesn't marry Bunny."

"You're kidding! How do you know that?"

"I was at the reading of Matt's will. At first, I had no idea why the attorney wanted me there, but it turned out it all had to do with the FFF audit that Matt wanted me to oversee. Bunny's not exactly being quiet about her opinion of the whole thing. Supposedly, she and Justin are engaged, although I guess it's unofficial because she's not wearing a ring, but she wants Justin to contest the will. He refused, and they had a big argument in the parking lot after they found out what was in the will. Oh, and one more tidbit: Bunny stands to inherit a million dollars if she doesn't marry Justin and leaves Iowa."

"Unbelievable! I love a romance, but I don't know Justin and Bunny well enough to have an opinion about whether or not they're meant to be together. I really think it should be their decision, though, not Matt's. Trying to control his son from the grave is just plain spooky."

"I don't know what will happen, but when we were shopping at Veronique's, I overheard Nancy telling Barb that she wanted to get away from the house for a while because of Justin's and Bunny's arguing. She seemed pretty stressed out."

"I can imagine, especially at a time like this. Poor Jennifer! I really don't want to go to Matt's funeral, but I'll go for Jennifer's sake. I have to keep telling myself that, as much as I disliked Matt, he wasn't all bad. He was a good board member, and FFF's benefiting in a big way from his bequest."

"True. I wonder why the anonymous tipster picked Matt as the person to warn. Of course, the tip could turn out to be bogus."

"I hope it does, but now that you mention it, I have an idea about who it might be."

Chapter 15

"I'm all ears. I guess if it's a legitimate tip, it must have come from one of FFF's staffers, but I have no idea who it could be. I just know it's not Marcie because she would have told the whole board about any problem, and she would have acted immediately. So who do think tipped Matt?"

"Well, this is just a guess, but it may have been our new intern, Chloe."

"I've never met her. To tell you the truth, I forgot that FFF had a new intern, but now that you mention it, I remember Marcie telling the board that Chloe would be working part-time and receiving some college credit for her internship. Why do you think Chloe's the one who tipped Matt?"

"Because I saw them talking outside the office a while back when I went by to drop off a few donation checks for FFF that my neighbors had given me. When Chloe and Matt saw me coming, they both looked startled and stopped talking right away. It just seemed odd at the time."

"Would an intern know enough about FFF's finances to learn there might be a problem?"

"It's possible. They usually let the interns do a little bit of everything. They pretty much have the run of the place."

"Hmm. Interesting. I guess it doesn't matter who tipped Matt off now that Dillon's conducting the audit. I just hope everything's in order."

"Me, too."

After Amy and I finished our conversation, I woke a sleepy Bear, and we both headed for the bedroom, where I fell asleep immediately.

The next thing I knew, my furry companion was nuzzling my arm, and it was already light outside. We'd both slept later than usual. I groaned as I rolled out of bed, still groggy from a sound sleep, and dawdled over a cup of coffee while Bear bounded around the backyard and rolled in the snow.

His energy exceeded mine, but I decided we might as well go for our walk now, so I hurriedly dressed, and we set off. The bright sunlight reflected off the snow, and I was happy I'd remembered to wear my sunglasses. We walked several blocks, waving as neighbors passed by in their cars, but we didn't encounter any other walkers until we reached the little park a couple blocks from Hawkeye Haven's community center. More of a garden than a park, there were tulip beds and some rose and peony bushes along with a few park benches. It was a good place to relax for a few minutes in warmer weather, but the ground was still covered by a foot of snow. The benches had been cleared, and a woman was sitting on one of them, her back to the street. Pulling at his leash, Bear started toward her. He was a strong boy, and when he wanted to go somewhere, it was sometimes difficult to hold him back.

"No, Bear!" I cautioned, tugging on his leash. The woman might not appreciate uninvited company.

She turned when she heard me, and I was surprised to see Jennifer, especially since this was the first time we'd ever encountered her during one of our daily walks.

"Hi, Laurel," she said, smiling wanly. "Come here, boy." Jennifer patted her knee, and Bear lurched forward. I didn't try to hold him back since Jennifer had encouraged him, but I hung onto his leash, just to be on the safe side. He'd been known to become distracted when he spotted a cat, a squirrel, or a rabbit. Jennifer petted Bear and scratched behind his ears while his body wiggled and his tail wagged. No doubt about it. Bear loved attention, and Jennifer gave him plenty.

"Why don't you join me, Laurel?" Jennifer said, shifting to one side of the park bench. I sat beside her while Bear lay down in front of us on a patch of sidewalk that had been cleared in front of the bench.

"Ooh, that looks cold," Jennifer said, "but he doesn't seem to mind."

"Most Labradors love cold weather, but below-zero temperatures are too much, even for Bear. I'm glad we're getting a break, even though I know winter's not over yet."

"Mmm."

I noticed that Jennifer seemed to drift off, so I didn't try to continue the conversation. We sat quietly for a few minutes, while an alert Bear lay at our feet, head up. I looked in the direction Bear was staring and saw a man across the street get into his car. When he drove off, Bear put his head down on his paws and closed his eyes.

"When I was a kid, I always wanted a dog, but we lived in an apartment, and my parents said a dog needed more space and a yard," Jennifer said, startling me. "After Justin was born, I suggested we get a dog. I thought a dog would make a great companion for a little boy, but Matt wouldn't hear of it," she continued, almost as though she were talking to herself. "He said a dog would chew on the furniture, make messes, and tear up the yard."

"Well, I can't deny that some dogs do all those things and more. Bear's a good boy, but he's quite a shedder. I'm constantly brushing him and vacuuming the house, but he's such a sweetie that he's worth it." I didn't exaggerate about his shedding. I was always on the lookout for stray Bear hairs on my clothing, so I kept lint brushes both in the house and in the car. I even had a mini-brush that fit in my smallest handbag. Somehow I couldn't imagine the perfectly-put-together Jennifer grooming a dog, but I was beginning to suspect that I didn't really know Jennifer very well.

"I guess I could get one now, couldn't I?" she said.

Again, I had the feeling that she was talking to herself, rather than to me, but I responded anyway. "Of course!"

"I might just do that," she said, "I really don't have any idea what I'm going to do." Tears seeped from her eyes, and she pulled a tissue out of her pocket and dabbed at them delicately.

"Jennifer, it's getting chilly sitting here. Why don't we go over to Alberto's and warm up with a cup of coffee?" Alberto's was the little restaurant situated in the same building that housed the pro shop for Hawkeye Haven's golf course. It was next to the community center where I taught my DIY classes. Alberto's had installed heaters on its patio, which was open on those rare winter days when the temperature was above forty degrees. Dogs were welcome on the patio, and Alberto's even had a special doggie menu of canine cuisine, although I hadn't allowed Bear to sample it because he'd been with me at Alberto's only for a quick coffee stop a few times. I always made him wait half an hour after his walk before feeding him in the morning.

"Yes, all right. I could do with a cup of coffee."

We reached Alberto's patio, going in through the gated side entrance, and found a few other residents breakfasting. One couple had a miniature dachshund with them in a stroller. It yipped at Bear, and he lurched toward the little dog, but I held him back. Bear liked to play with other dogs, but this was neither the time nor the place, and he was better suited to playing with a dog closer to his size, anyway. The small dachshund couldn't have weighed more than twenty pounds, and Bear weighed in at seventy pounds.

I waved at the dachshund's pet parents, and they waved back while Jennifer and I seated ourselves at a small table next to one of the heaters. The warmth felt good to me as I removed my gloves and held up my hands in front of the heater. Bear positioned himself as far away from the heater as possible and stretched out on the cement floor.

"Beautiful day, isn't it?" A brawny young man sporting a buzz cut, who looked as though he'd be more at home on a football field than waiting tables, continued without waiting for our answer. "Would you like to see a menu?"

"No, thanks. Just coffee for me. Jennifer?"

"I don't need a menu. I guess I'll have coffee, too," she said. "Wait! Do you have hot chocolate?"

"We sure do, and it's the best, made with whole milk, real cream—we get all our milk and cream fresh from a local dairy every day—Swiss chocolate, and whipped cream on top."

"That must have about a thousand calories," Jennifer commented.

As slender as Jennifer was, I figured she could probably afford a splurge once in a while, so her comment surprised me a little.

"I cannot tell a lie. You're right about that, but our hot chocolate is so good it's worth it."

"Well, it certainly sounds good. Okay. I'll have one."

After our server left, Jennifer confided that she hadn't drunk hot chocolate since she was a teenager.

"Really?"

"Really. I keep to a strict diet, and I count every calorie. Even when I was pregnant with Justin, I gained only what the doctor said I should and dieted back down to my regular weight as fast as I could."

"You have a lot more self-control than I have," I admitted. "How do you do it?"

"When we got married, Matt made me promise I'd never gain an ounce."

"Sounds like a lot of pressure to put on you."

"I guess it became a way of life eventually. I'm just starting to realize there's nobody around now who can tell me what to do." *Jennifer must have been firmly under Matt's thumb during her entire marriage*, I thought. "My husband was the ultimate control freak, but, in some ways, my life was easier because of it. I never had to worry about paying the bills, arranging for home repairs, or planning our vacations. I only had to do my job."

"You had a job?" I didn't think Jennifer had ever worked outside her home.

"My job was to look beautiful. I was Matt's arm ornament. That's what he wanted, but it became more and more difficult. I can't disguise my wrinkles any longer, and I have to exercise twice as long and twice as hard as I used to, just to get the same results. Matt was pushing me to get a face lift, and—I don't know—I just didn't want to do it, so I stalled. I consulted a plastic surgeon who actually recommended that I wait, but when I told Matt what he said, he wanted me to go to another doctor."

"I'm sorry, Jennifer." I didn't know what to say, but Jennifer just nodded and went on. Perhaps she needed someone to listen to her.

"I looked back on my life, and suddenly, it seemed so meaningless, except for having Justin, of course. What have I accomplished on my own?"

"You're a fabulous designer, Jennifer. You just won two design contests. Don't sell yourself short."

"You've always encouraged me, Laurel. I'd never have entered either of those contests if you hadn't thought I had a chance to win, but Matt complained that I shouldn't waste my time on silly competitions when I should be making arrangements to have a face lift. He made me so angry I just could have killed him." When she realized what she'd said, Jennifer put her hand over her mouth. "I really didn't mean that literally, Laurel; truly I didn't, but I knew then it was time for me to change my life. I consulted a lawyer about divorcing Matt. I didn't pursue it because Matt announced that he planned to have knee replacement surgery, and I felt I should wait. I have to admit I was terrified to tell him anyway. I'd thought about it for years, but I didn't want to disrupt Justin's life. Now that he's in college, perhaps it wouldn't have affected him so drastically, but I knew he wouldn't be happy about it, either."

"Ladies, your drinks," our server said, placing our cups carefully on the table.

"This looks delicious," Jennifer said, spooning blobs of whipped cream into her mouth. "Mmm. It is!"

"Jennifer, I'm sorry to hear about your troubles. You always seem so—" I struggled, trying to find the right words, "—so put together, so perfect."

"That's what Matt wanted. Even if I'd had the face lift, I don't think it would have been enough for Matt. I can't look like I'm nineteen again, no matter how much I try or how much plastic surgery I have." She sipped her hot chocolate, draining the cup. Then she leaned toward me and whispered, even though there was nobody sitting close enough to us to overhear our conversation. "I think Matt might have been seeing someone else, but I don't know for sure. I have to apologize again to you, Laurel, because when I came in and saw you at Anderson and Patton yesterday, the thought flashed in my mind that Matt might have left his girlfriend something and you might be the woman he was seeing."

"Wait a minute." I felt insulted. "How could you think that I would ever date another woman's husband?"

"I wasn't thinking straight. If I had been, I'd have realized that you're too old and that you're not Matt's type."

"Humph!" Now I felt doubly insulted.

"Oh, I don't mean. . ." she paused, probably realizing that the more she said, the worse her comments sounded. "Uh, look, I *know* you're not old. You must be seven or eight years younger than I am," she said appraisingly. "All I meant is that you're not nineteen, super skinny, and blond."

"Well, I guess you've got me there," I said, not quite sure how to react. I understood what she was trying to say, but I didn't much appreciate the way she said it.

"Really, Laurel, I admire you and all you've accomplished. I wish I hadn't dropped out of college when I married Matt, but he insisted there was no need for me to get a degree."

"You could go back to college now if you'd like."

"At forty-five? I don't know. I guess the real problem is I don't know what to do with the rest of my life. When I thought about divorcing Matt, I never thought beyond how relieved I'd feel not to have to live up to what he expected from me.

"I'm sorry, Laurel. I never meant to go on like this. I'm so mixed up, and I feel guilty for being angry with Matt for cutting Justin out of his inheritance. I told my lawyer I wanted to give my stock to Justin, but, evidently, it's not that simple. There are some stipulations about it that Mrs. Patton didn't go into yesterday morning.

"Then there's Bunny. She's been quite vocal about her opinion. She still wants Justin to contest Matt's will, and she's not wrong that the will's unfair. Justin and Bunny argued about it until late last night, and when she showed up early this morning, I couldn't take any more. I just had to get out of there for a while."

Jennifer's phone beeped, and she pulled it from her pocket to answer. "My mom," she mouthed to me.

I couldn't hear what Nancy was saying, but Jennifer's end of the conversation consisted mostly of "uh, huhs" and "all rights" before she said, "Alberto's" and hung up.

"Mom's going to pick me up in a few minutes. I guess she thinks I've been away from the house long enough." She signaled our server and asked him to put our drinks on Matt's tab. I didn't know Alberto's ran tabs for Hawkeye Haven's residents, but perhaps only certain residents were afforded the privilege.

"I'll walk out with you," I said. "Let's go, Bear." Bear jumped up, ready to resume his morning walk. When we reached the parking lot in front of Hawkeye Haven's community center, Nancy was pulling up in Jennifer's BMW.

Jennifer leaned toward me and murmured, "Please forgive me."

"It's all right. Take care of yourself," I said, gently patting her arm before she climbed into the passenger seat. Nancy acknowledged me with a wave before driving off.

"Well, Bear, what do you think of that?" Bear cocked his head and looked at me seriously as though he were considering his answer. As we walked back home, I thought about what Jennifer had told me. I'd learned more about her in the past hour than I'd known since I'd first met her when she enrolled in one of my jewelry-making classes a couple of years ago. Even so, something about Jennifer seemed off, but I couldn't put my finger on it.

Clearly, she was reeling from shock at the events of the past few days. I hadn't taken her words that she "just could have killed him" seriously, but how would they sound if revealed in courtroom testimony, especially since Jennifer stood to inherit a fortune when Matt died?

When Mrs. Patton detailed the terms of Matt's will, Jennifer had claimed she didn't know that Matt had made a new will. But what if that weren't true? What if she *had* known? Few motives for murder were more powerful than the desire for money.

On the other hand, if Jennifer wanted wealth so badly that she'd murder her own husband to inherit his money, she certainly hid it well. In fact, she'd also claimed amazement at the size of her husband's estate, and, if that were true, Jennifer hadn't ever realized that Matt was rich. Her worry about Justin and her uncertainty about her own life seemed to indicate that her concerns lay elsewhere, not with her inheritance.

In Jennifer's case, perhaps a stronger motive would be Matt's controlling behavior. Could Jennifer have simply snapped and taken the opportunity to smother Matt at a time when he'd had no control? Since she said she planned to divorce him, that scenario didn't make a lot of sense, especially because Jennifer's prize-winning pillow had been used by the killer. I knew how much she valued the beaded peacock pillow, so it was difficult to believe that she'd use it to do away with her husband.

I also found it hard to believe that the cool, calm, and collected Jennifer that I'd thought I knew could do such a thing, but I'd learned that, behind her facade, Jennifer's emotions churned, and she felt repressed from years under Matt's domination.

Still puzzled by Jennifer's behavior, I decided to ask Tracey's opinion about it the next time I talked to her. In the meantime, we'd arrive home soon, and it was time for me to focus on the tasks of the day. Although the first item on my to-do list, grocery shopping, wasn't my favorite, I determined to be more efficient than usual and make a complete list before going to Foster's.

Close to home, we were about ready to cross the street when a red Corvette suddenly screeched to a stop, blocking our way, and Justin jumped out, glowering furiously.

"What do you think you're doing?" he yelled.

Chapter 16

Justin started toward us, but Bear, on the alert, stopped in his tracks and growled at him, and Justin took a step back.

"I'm attempting to cross the street, and I'd appreciate it if you moved your car," I said, trying to keep my voice steady. Bear hadn't wavered from his guard stance.

"Hey, keep that dog back!"

"I will as long as you speak to me in a civil manner. What would your mother think?"

"You leave my mother out of this. This is between you and me."

"Justin, I really have no idea what you're talking about."

"I'm talking about the police dragging Bunny down to the station."

"What's that have to do with me?" I asked, although it dawned on me that Walker or Smith had probably asked Bunny to come in to revise her statement.

"Don't play coy with me. Bunny told me you asked her about seeing Edna asleep in the sunroom."

"Correction. I didn't ask Bunny anything until after she *volunteered* that she saw Edna in the sunroom. When she admitted that she hadn't told the police about it, I suggested that she should revise her statement. That's *all*."

"That's all? Don't you realize what you've done? The cops might think someone else killed dad while Edna was sleeping."

"Justin, I know you think Edna killed your father, and the police agree or she wouldn't be in custody right now. For argument's sake, though, let's just say they've arrested the wrong person. Don't you want justice for your father? What if the real killer's not in jail?"

Justin's face contorted in confusion. "Whoa! Wait a minute," he said, holding up his hand. "You really think there's a chance that Edna didn't do it?"

"Let's put it this way. If I had to sit on a jury, knowing only what I know now about Edna's case, I'd have to say there's a reasonable doubt. She may well have done it, but there's also a chance she didn't do it. More investigation may lead to more evidence, and you can't blame the police for collecting it. Surely, you want the district attorney to present the best case possible if this goes to trial." I deliberately avoided mentioning Bunny, but I couldn't help thinking that if Bunny had told Smith everything she knew when Smith took her statement the day of Matt's death, Walker might not have been so quick to arrest Edna.

"I still think Edna did it, but I guess more investigation couldn't hurt," Justin said grudgingly. At least, he'd calmed down enough that Bear had stopped growling.

"Maybe you should move your car, Justin. It's blocking the intersection, and I'd like to get home now."

"Okay." He seemed to deflate rather quickly. "I'm sorry I upset your dog," he mumbled although he didn't apologize for upsetting me.

He jumped back into the red Corvette, revved the engine, and took off, narrowly missing a fire hydrant as he executed a U-turn.

Before crossing the street, I stooped to hug Bear. "Good boy, Bear. You're a very good boy. You wanted to protect Mommy, didn't you?" I wasn't sure what Justin would have done if Bear hadn't been with me, and I didn't want to think about it. I was still shaking from the encounter.

Justin had shown another side of his personality. Now I knew he had an explosive temper that I'd never seen before. His father hadn't wanted him to date Bunny, and he'd done his best to try to prevent their marriage using the terms of his will. I suspected that, had Matt recovered from his knee surgery, he would have offered Bunny a similar large cash incentive to disappear, and Justin might not ever have been the wiser.

We'd been gone longer than I'd anticipated due to our unexpected visit with Jennifer, but I still had plenty of time to shop for groceries and work on the next design for my *DIY Perfect Pillows* book. I lingered over my coffee while I wrote an extensive grocery list. I fed Bear and I would have liked to have had a piece of toast or some cereal before I left for the grocery store, but I was out of both. By the time I'd filled my cart at Foster's, I'd worked up an appetite and couldn't resist buying some sugar cookies and a luscious cream cheese coffee cake when I passed the bakery section.

At home, I munched on a cookie while I put the groceries away and fed Bear some baby carrots. I'd been waiting for Wes to call with an update about his father's progress, but I hadn't heard from him, so I decided to call him. When I picked up my phone, I discovered that I'd forgotten to turn it on earlier, and Wes had left me a voice mail. I called him back immediately, apologizing for my oversight.

"Good timing. I need to take a break," he said when he answered my call.

"Are you at the hospital?"

"No. I'm pulling a few weeds at the house. My parents have a fairly big yard with desert landscaping. There's lots of gravel, flowering desert bushes, and cacti, but no grass, and weeds pop up through the gravel sometimes. Dad's worried about taking care of chores, so I promised him I'd remove the weeds and take his car into the shop for an oil change. He's especially obsessive about the cars. He'd planned to buy a new set of tires for mom's car the day he had the heart attack, and it's all he could talk about this morning, so I told him I'd take care of everything. That seemed to make him feel better, and it's making me feel better, too. Hanging around the hospital makes me restless, now that I know dad's going to recover."

"You're a man of action, so I'm not surprised."

"That's me." He laughed. "It's a relief to be doing something useful. The doctor's going to let us know this evening whether dad can come home tomorrow. If he does, I may be able to fly back on Monday. Denise still plans to stay another week or two to help."

"That sounds good. I can't wait to see you."

"I'll let you know for sure as soon as I find out what the doctor has to say. What's new in Hawkeye Haven?"

I told him about my encounter with Justin.

"I don't like the sound of that one bit. It's a good thing Bear was with you."

"Justin had calmed down, at least a little, by the time he took off, but I didn't appreciate what he did. I doubt that he would have done anything foolish, but it was scary at the time."

"That young man needs to learn some manners."

"I have a feeling Justin's been spoiled by his parents. Did I tell you they gave him a Corvette for his twentieth birthday? Red, no less."

Wes whistled. "That's some birthday present. I remember my first car. It was a beat-up old Chevy. I worked summers during high school so I could buy it."

"You never told me that. I didn't get my first car until after college. When I landed a job, I bought one on time. I still remember what a huge chunk of my paycheck went for car payments with another huge chunk going to pay on my student loan. Ah, the good old days."

"My good old days are even older than your good old days."

"Oh, Wes, you're not *that* old."

"Some days it feels like it, though. Seriously, when my dad had his heart attack, I couldn't believe it. I kept thinking he's not old enough to have a heart attack. Where did the time go?"

"All we can do is make the most of it."

"You're right, sweetheart. Well, these weeds won't pull themselves. I'd better get back to it. I'll call you tonight."

After we'd said our good-byes, I headed to my craft room, where I sketched the design for an appliquéd pillow that would be the next project in my book. Then I drew a pattern for the appliqué and chose the fabric from my stash of remnants.

Before I cut out the fabric, I remembered that I'd intended to order the semi-precious stones for the necklaces I'd promised to deliver to Veronique's by the end of next week, so I went to the office and grabbed my favorite supplier's catalog, setting it down in front of my computer so that I could flip the pages to the stones I needed, verify the item numbers, and enter them as I ordered online. Unfortunately, one of the stones I wanted was on back order. This happened rarely, which was one reason this particular jewelry-supply company was my go-to choice. The other reason was rapid shipping. It rarely took more than a few days before I received my order.

I began checking my list of back-up suppliers until I found one that had the stone beads I needed. I was checking their shipping schedule when I felt Bear's nose under my right forearm. He pushed it up. I put my arm back down again, poising my hands over the keyboard, and he nudged it again. This was his favorite trick when he wanted to get my attention while I was working on the computer. I pretended to ignore him, but he persisted.

I knew he'd never leave me alone until I figured out what he was after. He ran to the patio door in the den when I got up, so I let him outside and followed him, pulling on my coat and gloves. I looked for his hard rubber ball and found it next to a forlorn planter on the side of the patio. Thinking how happy I'd be when flowers bloomed in the planter, I threw the ball. Bear usually retrieved it and brought it back to me, but this time he jumped up and intercepted it before it hit the ground. It must have given him a bit of a jolt to catch it in his mouth, but he seemed unfazed as he ran to me, flipped his head, and released the ball. It landed at my feet. I scooped it up and threw it farther across the yard. Bear eagerly bounded through the snow and buried his nose in it to find his ball.

After we'd played fetch for longer than I wanted to but not long enough for Bear, I headed inside, and Bear reluctantly followed. If I hadn't stopped, he probably would have been happy to continue the game most of the afternoon, but I needed to get back to work. Tracey had invited us both to come over for an early dinner before she packed for her business trip, and I wanted to finish my beads order and my appliquéd pillow before we left.

I'd take notes as I made the pillow so that I could refer to them when I wrote the project instructions tomorrow. Bear cooperated nicely by snoozing while I worked, and I'd just put the final stitch in my pillow when my landline phone rang. I had an extension in my craft room. Before picking up the phone, I checked the caller ID, and when I saw who was calling, I answered right away.

"Hi, Dillon. I didn't expect to hear from you so soon."

"I didn't expect to have any news so soon, either, but I'm afraid that there's no doubt FFF has a big problem with the finances, and I've tracked down the source. You're not going to like this, Laurel, but the director's been embezzling funds from the organization going back to its beginning. All in all, she's stolen nearly two hundred thousand dollars over the past five years."

"Marcie?"

"Yes."

"But she founded FFF! I can't believe she'd do such a thing."

"She didn't do a very good job of hiding the embezzlement. She'd set up a couple of shell companies, supposedly consulting firms, and funneled the money through them. She's the sole owner of both companies."

"I'm stunned. She always seemed so dedicated to charity work. Why in the world would she do something like this?"

"Greed. I hate to say this, but I think she may have planned to take the money when she set up FFF as a non-profit organization. The first board members, including your current treasurer, were all people she'd dealt with at another agency where she handled public relations. That's what Roger told me. I suspect she chose them because they trusted her and wouldn't look too hard at the books."

"I guess we're all guilty of that. I never glanced twice at the treasurer's reports myself. I didn't realize he was a "treasurer in name only" as Matt indicated, but I can't just blame him. All of us, everybody on the board, should have been more responsible."

"You can't blame yourself, Laurel. You joined the board only a few months ago. The treasurer should have caught this problem early on, but he trusted Marcie, and so he didn't take more than a cursory look at the finances. He's kicking himself now for letting things go this far, but let's focus on the real culprit here because, unless FFF's board comes up with a viable plan to put the organization on solid footing, Mrs. Patton can withhold the donation and the money would revert back to Matt's estate, according to the terms of the will. Since the bequest amounts to far more than Marcie stole, it would behoove the board to act as soon as possible."

"Right. I understand we need to come up with a plan."

"May I suggest that you and Roger meet me at my office early tomorrow morning to formulate a strategy."

"Yes. I can be there at eight."

"Okay. Once we decide on a plan, I can run it by Mrs. Patton, and if it meets her approval, you and Roger can call an emergency board meeting."

"I didn't realize I could do that."

"Not alone. FFF's by-laws require two board members to call one, and a twenty-four-hour notice must be given."

"All right. I dread that board meeting, but thank you for acting so quickly, Dillon. I was really hoping you wouldn't find anything amiss."

"So was I. I'm sorry, Laurel. I know it's distressing, but try not to worry. We'll do our best to secure Matt's donation for FFF."

It was a good thing Dillon hadn't called until after I finished my project because I never would have been able to concentrate on it or anything else, knowing what Marcie had done. Because of her dishonesty, FFF could be in danger of losing a huge donation, and the organization could have contributed even more to our cause over the years if Marcie hadn't been siphoning off funds for her own benefit. I couldn't think of any possible excuse for her actions, especially since she'd evidently planned them right from the beginning.

Sensing my mood, Bear whimpered anxiously, so I sought to reassure him."

"It's okay, Bear. Mommy's okay."

"I stopped pacing to pet him and gave him a tummy rub. For the next hour, I busied myself with household chores, while Bear followed me from room to room until he tired of the routine and lay on his bed in the den, keeping a watchful eye on me as I mopped the kitchen floor.

When I finished, I took a quick shower and changed into jeans and a soft, comfy sweater. I'd offered to bring a dessert from Foster's, but Tracey had declined, saying she wanted to try a new brownie recipe. I knew she'd be whipping up an incredible dinner. Crazy as it seemed to me, Tracey really considered cooking and baking relaxing. I always said she got the cooking genes in the family.

I packed Bear's dinner in a plastic container, stowed it in a large tote along with my handbag and cell phone, and put on my winter parka and gloves. Sensing that something was up, Bear pranced around the kitchen, his tail whipping back and forth. As soon as I grabbed his leash, he ran to me and nudged my hand. I snapped the leash on his collar, turned the hall light on, and we went to the garage where our chariot awaited. After Bear jumped into the back seat, we were off, observing Hawkeye Haven's painfully slow fifteen-mile-per-hour speed limit for the mile drive to Tracey's house.

Light from the street lamps and Tracey's porch reflected off the snow in her front yard. Her sidewalks were shoveled and the snow cleared from her driveway, where I parked. As soon as I opened the car door, Bear jumped out, rushing ahead of me in his eagerness to see Tracey. He didn't get too far because I had a firm grip on his leash. When he stopped, he turned to look at me as if to say "hurry up."

Tracey opened the front door just as we reached it. "Come in!"

Bear paused long enough for a quick hug from Tracey before barreling into the kitchen, where he knew Tracey had stashed a treat. Whenever we visited her, she always put out a bowl for Bear with a homemade treat. Tracey's offering this evening was one of Bear's favorites, crispy yam chips, which he gobbled up immediately.

"You'll never guess what I've made for dinner," Tracey said.

"Probably not, but how about a clue?"

Chapter 17

"It's an Iowa specialty."

"Hmm. It can't be corn on the cob because we're in the middle of winter, and you would never serve sweet corn unless it was grown locally, so I'm going to say it must be something you made with the corn you canned last summer."

"Bzzz. Wrong! That's a good guess, though. It's my version of an Iowa pork tenderloin sandwich. The traditional version is deep fried, but mine's pan fried."

"Yummy! I'm starving. I didn't have any lunch today."

"Well, sit down and dig in," Tracey said, as she drained the smashed, coated tenderloins on some paper towels and assembled our sandwiches. "I have German potato salad, baked beans, and the last of the watermelon pickles I made last summer."

"Delicious," I said, as I bit into my sandwich. Bear had followed Tracey to the kitchen table. He looked at me and whined softly until I realized I'd forgotten to give him his dinner. Once I'd done that, he lay contentedly at our feet while we finished our dinner and indulged in the minty brownies Tracey had made.

"When do you leave for Dallas?" I asked.

"The flight's tomorrow morning, and we're due back on Wednesday. I hate funerals, so the trip's giving me a legit excuse not to attend Matt's. I called Jennifer this morning to explain, but she wasn't home, so her mom took the message."

I filled Tracey in on the reason Jennifer hadn't been

home and the revelations she'd shared with me. Then I told her about my encounter with Justin and Bear's reaction to Justin's aggressive behavior. I wrapped up with a summary of what Dillon had discovered when he audited FFF's books.

"Marcie's an embezzler? Our book club Marcie? That's hard to believe!"

"Isn't it awful? I'm still having trouble believing it myself, but I know how thorough Dillon is. He says her embezzlement scheme was rather amateurish, at best."

"I'm flabbergasted. Whenever she came to our book club, she always talked about all the good FFF does in Center City. She seemed so sincere."

"You know, I've been thinking about that, and I wouldn't be surprised if she's excusing herself on the grounds that FFF does a lot of good for the community. Maybe she feels she's entitled to a bigger cut, although her salary's hardly paltry. She's the only person on the FFF staff who's being paid the going rate, as far as salary's concerned."

"Surely she must realize by now that she can't get away with it anymore. When she first heard about the audit, she must have been petrified."

"She sure didn't act like it at the time, although she kept asking me to let her help. You can imagine what assistance she would have given me. I think she figured if she could put it off a little longer, she'd have time to cover her tracks. If she could have somehow manipulated the outcome of the audit, she could have continued on her merry way with an extra five million dollars in FFF's bank account. It's a lot of money. Maybe she wanted to get her hands on some of it so much that she deluded herself into thinking she could outsmart a trained auditor."

"I'm still having trouble wrapping my mind around it. I was sitting next to a criminal at our book club, and

I didn't even realize it."

"You know something else? She didn't learn about the donation in Mrs. Patton's office like the rest of us. She *knew* Matt had changed his will. She already knew about the five million."

"Are you sure?"

"Pretty sure. She told Josh, her assistant, about it before Matt died."

"I think I see where you're going with this."

"She had a motive. She could have gone through the back door of the powder room and into the downstairs bedroom. She could have smothered Matt with Jennifer's pillow and come right back to our book discussion."

"You're right. She may have had time to do it, but I don't remember her being gone very long. I wish I could remember more clearly."

"I wish I could, too, but why would we? We were at Jennifer's for our book club. We had no idea her husband would be murdered practically under our noses."

"Embezzlement's bad enough, but murder, too? Do you really think Marcie's capable of killing?"

"I don't know. I wouldn't have thought she was capable of embezzlement, but now I know better."

We sipped our coffee in silence for a few minutes, each lost in our own thoughts. I helped myself to another brownie, chewing it slowly and savoring its chocolaty goodness.

"Tracey?"

"Umm."

"You're the dating expert. I want to ask you something."

"Uh, oh. Trouble in paradise?"

"No. At least, I don't think so. It's just something Wes said."

"Out with it."

"Okay. Wednesday evening when Wes came over, he said that he hoped all his late hours and our postponed dates weren't going to be a problem. I assured him that I understood, but he's brought it up several times. I mean, of course, I'm disappointed when we have to cancel our plans, but I know he has a job to do. I don't expect him to neglect work so that he can take me to the movies. Why do you think he keeps bringing it up?"

"You two certainly look solid to me, so I wouldn't read too much into it. Two things: I think he wants to be positive that you're okay with his schedule, and I think it's possible his long hours may have been an issue in a previous relationship. That could be the reason he wants to make absolutely sure that you can live with all his overtime."

"I see what you mean. He's never mentioned anyone else, other than his ex-wife. I know she didn't want him to stay on the police force, but her objection may have had more to do with his salary than his hours. That was nearly twenty years ago, though."

"That might have something to do with it, or maybe a more recent relationship."

"Should I ask him?"

"I wouldn't. Just keep doing what you're doing. He doesn't bring it up constantly, does he?"

"No. Just once in a while."

"In that case, Dear Tracey says you're good to go. Just relax and have fun. You two make a great couple."

"You think?"

"Definitely! Now who needs reassurance?"

As Bear and I drove home, I smiled thinking about Tracey's advice to me. Several months ago, when I first met Wes, I'd asked Tracey's advice, and she hadn't steered me wrong. I felt better now because I'd worried that Wes might think we had a problem, but, based on what Tracey had said, it seemed more likely that he felt a bit insecure. I resolved to do my best to assure him that I could live with his schedule and that his job wouldn't be an issue in our relationship. When he called later that evening, I was happy to learn that his dad would be discharged from the hospital tomorrow. If all went well, Wes would be on a flight home Monday.

Pleasant as our hour-long conversation had been, when I went to bed, I couldn't help thinking about the meeting at Dillon's office the next morning and the inevitable upcoming confrontation with Marcie. I spent a restless night and woke feeling unsettled. I wasn't looking forward to dealing with FFF's financial problems, but it had to be done.

After a quick walk with Bear, I showered, dressed, and fed Bear his breakfast. When I put my coat on, Bear looked at me with his big brown eyes as if to say, "don't leave me, Mommy," but I knew he'd settle down after I left. When it came to laying a guilt trip on me, my dog was a true champ.

As I backed my car out of the driveway, I saw the colonel leaving Liz's. Putting my window down, I called to him that I wouldn't forget to feed Miss Muffet her dinner, said I hoped Liz's plane would land on time, and wished him a good trip to Omaha. I could tell he was eager to get on his way, and I didn't want to be late for the meeting at Dillon's office, so I didn't tarry.

I arrived at Dillon's office with five minutes to spare before our meeting. I hadn't even taken time for my usual morning coffee, so when Dillon's receptionist offered me a cup, I accepted gratefully. Roger and Dillon walked in together a few minutes later, and we all headed to Dillon's office.

We looked at each other solemnly before Roger broke the ice.

"I don't know about you," he said, looking at me,

"but I barely slept a wink last night thinking about Marcie's embezzlement. To say I'm disappointed in her would be putting it mildly. I can't believe she'd do such a thing, but Dillon knows his stuff. I've seen the evidence, and it's conclusive."

"I'll have the full final report ready to present to the board by tomorrow morning," Dillon said. "I can present my findings to the board, if you'd like, but, otherwise, it's up to you and the other board members to make a decision about how you want to handle it. As I suggested yesterday, it would probably be a good idea to go in with a viable plan that Mrs. Patton would approve; otherwise, FFF stands to lose the entire five-million-dollar bequest. However, it's up to the board to make any decisions. You may want to consult FFF's attorney since I'm acting in my capacity as an auditor."

"I don't think that's necessary, Dillon," Roger said. "FFF doesn't have an attorney on retainer. The last time we needed any legal advice was when the non-profit was set up five years ago."

"I agree," I said. "The board should be able to handle this. Marcie's committed a crime, and we have every right to report her to the police and insist that the district attorney prosecute her, but I worry that FFF's reputation could be so badly damaged that community donations dry up. If that happens, even Matt's bequest won't be enough to keep FFF going indefinitely."

"You make a good point, Laurel, but we can't let her get off without any consequences. She should have to pay back the money," Roger said.

"That's a lot of money, but I doubt that she has much of it left," I said. "She's always talking about all the vacations she takes, and I know her clothes and jewelry didn't come cheap," I said.

"If that's the case, once she loses her job at FFF, she'd have no way of paying back the money, and she may not be able to find another job without a recommendation from FFF," Dillon commented. "By the way, the statute of limitations for embezzlement on this scale is three years. Since I don't practice criminal law, I didn't know that myself until I looked it up. If she agrees to restitution, but fails to provide it, you won't be able to have criminal charges brought after three years."

"I don't think it's likely that she'll ever repay the entire amount she stole," Roger said, "but I have an idea that just might get partial repayment for FFF while avoiding a public scandal. Let me excuse myself to make a phone call, and then I'll run it by you, and you can tell me what you think."

"Roger seems like a new man," I said when he left the room, "a man on a mission."

"He thinks he could have stopped Marcie in her tracks if he'd been paying attention to FFF's finances. He trusted her, and she took advantage of his trust."

"I guess the same goes for everybody on the board. Marcie's honed her public relations skills and fundraising ability to perfection. She fooled a lot of people."

"That she did," Dillon agreed. "More coffee, Laurel? I'm going to grab a cup while Roger's on the phone."

"Yes, please. Black's fine."

Dillon disappeared for a few minutes before returning with two mugs of steaming coffee. I wasn't feeling as sharp as I would have liked due to the lack of sleep the night before, but I felt more alert after my second cup.

"Here's what I've come up with," Roger said when he came back into the office and settled himself into one of Dillon's plush chairs. "My son in Los Angeles manages and promotes musicians. He tells me several of the groups he works with are big-name talents, but since my musical tastes run to old show tunes, I wouldn't recognize any of them myself." When Roger mentioned the names of a couple of rock groups, Dillon looked almost awestruck.

"Both of those bands are huge!" he exclaimed. "I'm a big fan."

Roger smiled and nodded. "Okay. Well, then, Eric's willing to do his old man a favor by hiring Marcie for public relations work. If she has a job, she can pay restitution to FFF. Naturally, she wouldn't have anything to do with the management side of things, so she won't be able to manipulate any accounts. He said he'd make sure his controller goes over all the expenses she submits for reimbursement with a fine-tooth comb, but only Eric and his controller will know the reason. Eric's willing to take her on because I explained how talented she is at PR."

"So you're proposing to let her skate on any embezzlement charges and have her agree to a repayment plan?" I asked.

"That's the idea. What do you think?"

"It would certainly preserve FFF's reputation in the community, and we could get at least some of the money back, I suppose, but wouldn't it take forever for her to pay it all back?" I asked.

"I figure about five years, based on the salary she'll receive," Roger said. "Of course, after three years have elapsed, we won't have much of a hold on her...."

"What if she doesn't want to take the job? I assume she'd have to move to Los Angeles."

Roger shrugged. "It's in her best interests to leave town, if you ask me, and if she doesn't agree to take the position and can't make restitution some other way, I think we should turn over our evidence to the police and let the district attorney do his job."

"It sounds like a solid plan. It makes me angry that

she's put us in this position, but we need to move forward," I said.

"All right. Are you ready for me to speak with Mrs. Patton to make sure she'll approve this approach? I suspect it won't be a problem since Mr. Daniels obviously wanted the money to go to FFF, and by handling the situation, you're taking care of the financial problem as best you can."

Roger and I both nodded. We waited while Dillon called Mrs. Patton, gave her the results of the audit, and asked whether she'd approve our proposed plan. She tentatively agreed pending FFF's board approval and Marcie's signing off on a repayment plan.

"It looks like we're in business then," Roger said. "I'd like to get this board meeting scheduled as soon as possible. How about ten tomorrow morning?"

"That's fine with me." I said. "Matt's funeral will be at one tomorrow, but if we schedule our board meeting at ten, we should have enough time to take care of business before we go to the funeral. I assume all the board members will be attending."

"I'm sure they will. Let's send out the notice for the emergency meeting right away."

"Yes. I think it would also be a good idea for us each to contact individual board members and let them know the score before the meeting. That should speed things up, too."

"Agreed," Roger said, and we decided which board members we'd each contact before I sent out the email message via my phone saying that Roger and I were calling an emergency board meeting. We thanked Dillon, said we'd see him at the board meeting, and left to make our phone calls.

By noon, I'd spoken to Amy and one other board member. The third member on my contact list didn't answer, so I left a voice mail. Because Marcie was board president, she had to be notified as well, but since Roger asked for her to be on his list, I didn't plan on talking to her until the board meeting. I thought Roger would probably tell her what he had in mind so that she'd be ready to accept his proposal.

Marcie had hoped to bury the facts if I agreed to let her help me with the audit details, but she knew that she'd be exposed as an embezzler as soon as I showed up at FFF's office with Dillon and Roger. Relying on her bubbly personality and skill in public relations to get her out of the jam wouldn't work this time, so I wondered how she planned to handle our discovery of her duplicity.

As I was thinking about Marcie, my home phone rang. Assuming that the board member I couldn't reach earlier was calling me back, I picked up.

"It's about time! Where have you been?" an angry voice demanded.

"Who is this?"

"Who do you think it is? It's Edna. I want to know why I'm still stuck here at the detention center. I thought you were such a hotshot detective. Why haven't you found out who the real killer is yet?"

Chapter 18

"Edna," I said, exasperated, "I already explained to you that I'm not a private investigator, and you're not helping yourself by badgering me."

"So you *do* know something," she said accusingly, "and you're holding back. Why? So you can have a Perry Mason moment when you announce who really murdered Matt?"

"Don't be ridiculous!"

"It's not fair," she whined, switching tactics. "I did *not* smother Matt, but I'm the one sitting in jail. Can't you hurry up and find out who killed him? Please."

"Edna, you have to admit that you had a motive."

"No, I didn't!"

"Come on. I found out about your son. You blamed Matt for reporting him to the police when he burglarized Matt's house."

"I blamed Matt five years ago. Not now. Jacob's been in trouble since he turned thirteen. If it hadn't been Matt who turned him in, it would have been someone else. Jacob was living with me, but I couldn't control him. He was becoming more aggressive every day. He even hit me a few times. I hate to say it, but he may be better off in prison than on the outside."

Although Edna sounded sincere, I had my doubts.

"That's a harsh statement, considering you're talking about your own son."

"I know it, but it's the truth," she said with a sigh. "If that's the reason you still think I did it, you'd better think again." With that, she hung up on me, leaving me to wonder just what the truth was. With Edna, I never really knew.

After I took Bear outside for playtime, I got down to work. I hadn't made nearly as much progress on my *DIY Perfect Pillows* manuscript as I'd hoped during the past week, and I wouldn't have any time to work on it tomorrow, what with the board meeting and Matt's funeral. I vowed to double up on my project production as soon as possible.

Jennifer had texted me and the other book club members, inviting us to her home after the funeral. She said the gathering would be limited to family, friends, and close neighbors. If she had a public reception after the funeral, she and Justin would have to contend with hundreds of mourners, since Matt had been a prominent businessman, well known not only in Center City, but also in the entire state of Iowa.

Poor Jennifer! Despite Justin's rude behavior toward me, I felt sorry for him, too. I thought the shock of learning the terms of his father's new will only days after his father's murder was proving more than Justin could handle, and his girlfriend's pressuring him to contest the will made his stress even more unbearable.

Wes had called to let me know that his father had been released from the hospital and was comfortably ensconced in his favorite lounge chair, watching a DVD of an old John Wayne movie. Since his father was home and doing well, Wes had booked a flight to return to Des Moines tomorrow.

I wanted to pick him up at the airport, but he insisted that he had some business to take care of before returning to Center City and that his brother-in-law would bring him home. Since his flight would be landing at the same time Matt's funeral started, I didn't press the matter. We made plans to go to dinner in the evening after he got back.

Soon, the insistent beeping of the timer on my oven reminded me to go next door to feed Miss Muffett. Since Bear and Miss Muffett didn't get along, I left him home, telling him mommy would be back soon. Liz and I kept keys to each other's houses for just such occasions. I know Miss Muffett heard me come in, but she didn't present herself, preferring to hide under the bed. Hoping I could lure her out, I made more noise than necessary, rattling her cat food in her bowl before I set it down in the kitchen. Since that didn't entice her, I decided I should leave her alone. I turned up the thermostat to seventy-five degrees, as the colonel had requested, and I also turned on Liz's porch light and two lamps in the living room before returning to the kitchen to refresh Miss Muffet's water.

I heard voices outside, and before I could open the front door for them, Liz and the colonel burst in.

"Liz!" I exclaimed, hugging her, "welcome home." We air kissed as usual, since I didn't want to disturb her perfect make-up. She didn't look like a woman who'd been traveling all day. Every hair was in place, and her long, beaded, blue floral tunic draped beautifully over her dark blue leggings. She wore stylish short boots with heels higher than I would ever wear, and I marveled once again at her dramatic sense of style. Not many eighty-year-olds could have carried it off, but Liz was an exception.

"It's great to be back. I guess I came home in the eye of the hurricane, so to speak. Bobby says the thaw's predicted to last one more day, and then another snowstorm's going to hit." Whenever Liz called the colonel Bobby, I wondered if she was the only one he permitted to call him by his nickname. The first time I met him, he'd introduced himself as Colonel Robert Forrester Gable, but the first time he met Liz, he asked her to call him Bobby. I know because I was there.

Suddenly a fluffy ball of fur sped through the living room and hurtled into Liz's arms. She cradled Miss Muffett and cooed to her in kitty speak.

"What a surprise! Miss Muffett usually snubs me when I return home after a trip," Liz said as she stroked the persnickety Persian.

"That's the first time I've seen her since you left," the colonel told Liz. "Whenever I show up to feed her, she disappears, but the food's always gone by the next meal. She doesn't take to anybody but you."

"Poor Muffy," Liz murmured. "I've neglected you shamefully, haven't I?"

The cat batted at Liz's arm as if to say she agreed, and we all chuckled.

"That cat has you wrapped around her little paw," the colonel said, and I had to agree. Of course, Bear had me wrapped around his big paw, so I knew all about pampered pets.

"I'm so glad you're back home, Liz," I said, "although you'll probably be missing the Florida weather very soon. I should get going now. Will I see you at the funeral tomorrow?"

Liz nodded. "We'll be there."

"Would you like to ride with us?" the colonel asked.

"Thank you, but I better take my own car. I have to attend a meeting first and probably won't have time to come home afterwards. I'll go straight to the funeral from there."

We said our goodbyes, but I didn't hug Liz again. Miss Muffett could be fierce, and I didn't want to disturb her.

The next morning, I steeled myself for the board meeting. I dreaded seeing Marcie. Learning about her embezzlement had completely changed my feelings toward her. I thought about what an awkward situation the board meeting presented, but then I wondered whether Marcie would show up at all. Knowing that she'd been found out, maybe she'd opt to skip it so that she wouldn't have to face the board members. I was half-hoping she'd decided not to appear when I pulled into the parking lot at the strip mall where FFF's board offices were located, and I saw Marcie climbing the steps.

I waited in my car until she'd gone inside; then, I took a deep breath and followed. The outer office was deserted. I went to the conference room and found the other board members already seated around the table. Dillon was sitting next to Roger. As vice-president of FFF's board, Amy would conduct the meeting. She sat at the head of the table, Marcie's usual spot, and I took the place on her right side.

"Where's Marcie?" I whispered to Amy. "I saw her come into the outer office."

"I don't know. She can't be in her private office because Roger had the locks changed yesterday, and she doesn't have the key."

Just then, Marcie strode in, gave Amy a withering look, and plopped in the chair at the opposite end of the table. A couple of the board members actually looked away.

Amy announced the start of the emergency meeting and deferred to Roger, who asked Dillon for a summary of his audit report. Since everyone had been forewarned about the reason for the meeting, we all knew what was coming. After Dillon concluded his report, Roger asked Marcie if she wished to make a statement.

"FFF wouldn't be here if it weren't for me. I started it, and I have the right to run it as I see fit."

"That's not the case, Marcie," Amy said. "The board governs this organization. You may be president of the board, but as FFF's executive director, you're also an employee, and you've failed miserably in your duty.

That ends immediately. Your services are no longer required."

"Who's organized everything from the very beginning? Who does the lion's share of the work whenever we put on an event to raise funds? Who convinced Matt Daniels to leave FFF a huge donation? Me, that's who. You people are only here to rubber stamp whatever *I* decide to do."

"I don't see any rubber stamps here today," I said, looking around the room. "You've committed a crime, Marcie. We'd be within our rights to turn over our auditor's report, along with the supporting evidence, to the police and insist that the district attorney prosecute you. You could end up in jail."

"What? That's crazy. I didn't hurt anyone."

"You may not have hurt anyone physically, but you certainly hurt our clients, all the people we help. The money you stole could have gone to buy food for them," Roger said.

Marcie crossed her arms, leaned back in her chair, and stared straight ahead, giving Amy an uncomfortable moment, but Amy didn't look away. I passed a note to Roger, asking him whether he'd talked to Marcie since our meeting in Dillon's office. He shook his head. So Marcie didn't even know about the plan he'd hatched. I surmised that she'd deliberately avoided his calls. We still had to decide our course of action officially, which meant the board had to vote. If Marcie continued to act defiant, rather than contrite, the outcome could be far different than the one Roger and I had discussed yesterday morning in Dillon's office.

"Are you sure you want to continue to insist that you didn't do anything wrong when we have irrefutable proof that you did?" Don, the board member who hadn't been able to attend the FFF gala because he had the flu, asked.

Marcie didn't reply.

"Marcie, there's a way forward for you if the board approves it, a way you can avoid prosecution, " Roger said mildly.

"No, I don't want to hear about it, you old goat," Marcie yelled and stood up. She pointed her finger at Roger. "If you'd been doing your job, none of this would have happened. It's all your fault!" She turned and flounced out of the conference room, slamming the door on her way.

Stunned at her reaction, we looked at each other before we all started talking at once. The babble hadn't died down when Amy tapped the gavel to get our attention.

"Please, one at a time. We're not getting anywhere this way. Let's go around the table so that each person can have a say." Order restored, the board members, each in turn, voiced their opinions. It was a mixed bag. Since Marcie hadn't shown any remorse or offered to make restitution, some favored criminal prosecution. Others pushed for a civil suit, although, admittedly, a lawsuit against Marcie to recover the money she'd embezzled could turn out to be a very costly affair with no guarantee of restitution, even if FFF won. Roger and I both thought we should try to convince Marcie to take the job in California that Roger's son offered her and sign an agreement to pay FFF back.

"What if we do this," Amy said, hoping to break the deadlock. "Let's give Roger and Laurel forty-eight hours to contact Marcie and try to work something out. If she won't agree, we can vote on our next step at our regular board meeting. How does that sound?"

In the time-honored tradition of groups who were having trouble arriving at a decision, we agreed to put it off, just as Amy suggested. Roger and I walked out together.

"That didn't go very well," Roger said, "but maybe it's not too late to talk some sense into Marcie and maintain FFF's good reputation. I think I'll stop by her house before the funeral and try to talk to her. Maybe we both could go."

"We don't have much time before the funeral," I said. "Let me try. I know her from our book club, and she lives in Hawkeye Haven, too. Since I'm a resident there, I can go right through the resident's gate without stopping to get a pass from the guard. Besides, I'm the one Matt designated to oversee the audit and resolve any problems. I feel responsible."

"All right," Roger agreed. "She might listen to you. She must be starting to realize what a tight spot she's in. I'll be anxious to hear what she says."

Roger wasn't the only one who felt anxious. As I drove back to Hawkeye Haven, my stomach did flip-flops. Since our book club had met once at Marcie's house, I knew exactly where she lived. I parked and walked to her front door. Her car wasn't in the driveway, but that wasn't unusual since Hawkeye Haven's HOA decreed that cars should be parked in their owners' garages. What was unusual was that Marcie's drapes were drawn in midday. I rang the doorbell. When she didn't answer, I knocked loudly, but she still didn't come to the door. I wasn't ready to give up yet.

Tramping through the snow, I went around the side of her house and tried the gate to the back yard. I pushed it open and trudged through more snow on the patio. Marcie's patio door was covered by closed vertical blinds. I tried to peek inside, hoping for a glimpse between the slats, but I couldn't see a thing. In a last-ditch effort, I pounded on the patio door. With all the noise I was making, I didn't hear the footsteps.

"Freeze! Don't make a move!"

Chapter 19

Startled by the brusque command, I jumped back, losing my balance and landing on my backside in the snow. The tall man with sandy hair standing over me was Luke, Hawkeye Haven's head of security.

"Laurel? What in the world?" he exclaimed, extending his hand to help me up. "Are you hurt?"

"Just my pride," I said ruefully, dusting off the back of my coat off. "What are you doing here?"

"Security got a call from a neighbor saying someone was trying to get into Marcie's house. I happened to be right down the street in the rover, so I said I'd check it out myself. Is there a problem?"

"I need to talk to Marcie about urgent FFF business, but she doesn't seem to be home." What I didn't say was that I thought she might very well be home, hiding in her house so that she didn't have to speak to me. "It's really important."

"Must be for you to be pounding on her back door. If you have any reason to believe she's hurt, I'll call the police for a welfare check."

"No. I don't really think that's necessary. I saw her earlier this morning, but I thought she'd be home now. Maybe she's already gone to the funeral."

"Mr. Daniels' funeral, right?"

"Yes. I guess I'd better go. Maybe I can catch up with her there."

By the way Luke was looking at me, I could tell he thought my story was a mite fishy, but he didn't comment, as we walked back around the house.

Although I'd told Luke that Marcie might have already gone to the funeral, I very much doubted she'd have the nerve to show up there. When I arrived at the church, its parking lot was jammed, and cars were parked on the street for a couple blocks around it. I found the closest spot I could and walked hurriedly toward the church. At the first intersection, I was joined by a familiar-looking, red-faced woman coming from a side street.

"Hello, again," she said. "Didn't I see you bringing food to the Danielses' house a few days ago?" As soon as she mentioned the food, I remembered her as one of Jennifer's neighbors who'd stopped to chat with me that afternoon.

"Yes. That's right. I'm Laurel McMillan. I was so distracted by the cold weather that I don't think I properly introduced myself the other day."

"Nice to see you again, Laurel. I'm Fiona, Fiona Casey. My husband had to work today, so I came on my own. Do you live in Hawkeye Haven, too?"

"Yes. I moved here three years ago from Seattle. Have you lived here long?"

"Oh, my, yes. We bought our house new from the builder, so it's been about twenty years now. Jennifer and Matt have lived in the neighborhood almost that long. I remember Justin was a toddler when they moved in."

"So I guess you've known Edna a long time, then?"

"At least ten years, and I'll tell you something else. I still don't think she killed Matt. She's always been a good neighbor to us."

"I talked to Edna, and she says she didn't do it, but the police think she has a motive. She argued with Matt about five years ago—something about her son." I didn't know how much Fiona knew, but I was hoping the garrulous woman would want to talk about it.

"That awful son of hers. She really tried to keep him in line, but it was impossible. He's right where he belongs now, if you ask me." She lowered her voice and confided, "Jacob used to hit her, his own mother, if you can believe it. I even saw him do it once, and I threatened to call the police, but Edna begged me not to. She used to try to hide the bruises with sunglasses and a big brimmed hat, but that didn't fool me."

"That's terrible," I said. So Edna had told me the truth after all.

By this time, we'd reached the church. The sidewalk outside teemed with people on their way to Matt's funeral. A woman in a short faux fur coat beckoned to Fiona, and Fiona called to her that she'd join her in a minute. Fiona invited me to sit with her and her friend, but I told her I planned to meet my neighbor.

I stayed outside surveying the area, looking for someone I knew to come along. After about five minutes, I spotted Amber and a young woman making their way through the crowd. As they came closer, I noticed that the girl looked like a younger version of Amber with the same good looks, blond hair, and lithe body, not that Amber was old herself. At twenty-five, she was the youngest member of our book club. Sidling through the throng, I met them at the bottom of the church steps.

"Hi, Laurel," Amber said. "I think you know my cousin Chloe."

I shook my head. "No, but I'm about to. Hi, Chloe. I'm Laurel."

Chloe bobbed her head up and down. "I know," she said. "I've seen you at the FFF office, but we've never met. I work there part-time."

"Oh, right. You're the new intern."

"Yes. Marcie suggested that everybody in the office attend the funeral, but I was planning to skip it until

Bunny insisted I show up and come over to Matt's house afterwards."

"Maybe we should go in now so that we can find a seat. It looks really crowded," Amber said.

We climbed the short flight of steps to the front doors of the church, which were standing open. Two ushers, one on each side, were handing out memorial programs to the mourners as they entered the church. Another usher led us up the aisle and indicated a half-empty pew, where we could sit. I slid in first, followed by Amber, while Chloe sat on the end. Glancing at the program, I saw a handsome photo of Matt on the front. Inside was a glowing biography, and on the facing page, the program for the funeral. The names of three speakers were listed, one of whom I didn't recognize. The other two were Marcie and Justin. I realized that Jennifer didn't know about the embezzlement and that she must have arranged for Marcie to speak days ago.

While the organist played solemn music, the mourners spoke to each other in hushed voices as they waited for the funeral service to begin. When a rock tune burst out, the people around us turned toward an embarrassed Chloe, who had forgotten to turn off her cell phone when we entered the church. She mouthed "sorry" and carried out a short conversation in whispers before she told us that Bunny wanted Chloe to come up front to sit with her.

"I don't really think I should be there, but Bunny won't take 'no' for an answer. I'll see you later."

After Chloe left, I whispered to Amber, "How does Chloe know Bunny? They don't seem to have much in common."

"They were in high school together, and last semester, they were both in the same math class at the community college, but Chloe says they've never been close friends. She was surprised when Bunny

practically begged her to be here. Bunny told her
Justin's family hates her, and she wanted to have a
friend with her today."

The organ music stopped, and the pastor began the
service. After prayers and hymns, the pastor spoke of
Matt's life and then called on the first speaker, one of
his partners in Iowa Insurance Plans. I held my breath
as the man finished. According to the program, the next
speaker was Marcie. Instead, one of FFF's board
members, Don, appeared, saying that he was subbing
for Marcie, who was "indisposed." Speaking about
Matt's devotion to FFF and his generous donation to the
charity, Don did a creditable job with his talk,
considering that he'd obviously been pressed into
service at the last moment when Marcie didn't show up.

I felt so sick about Marcie and the way she'd put
FFF in jeopardy that I had trouble concentrating during
the rest of the service. After I'd left her house, I'd tried
to call her, but my calls had gone straight to voice mail.
I wondered again if she'd been home but in hiding
when I knocked on her door. If she continued to refuse
to cooperate, we'd have an even bigger mess on our
hands, and I feared FFF might not survive the scandal.

Matt's casket was open in the front of the church,
and many of the mourners were filing by and exiting
through a side door, but neither Amber nor I felt
inclined to view Matt's body. Although I realized the
custom might be somewhat comforting to others, I
found it upsetting, so when the service ended, Amber
and I walked out through the front door together. We
didn't wait for Chloe because she'd texted Amber that
she would be riding to Matt's house with Bunny.

Outside, I took in several deep breaths of fresh, cool
air. The church had been filled with dozens of floral
arrangements, so much so that the cloying scent of all
the funeral bouquets had almost overwhelmed me.

"I'm glad that's over," Amber said. "I hate funerals. I'm going over to the house because Jennifer invited us, but it's so heartbreaking. I parked down there," Amber said, pointing to the right. "Where are you parked?"

I pointed in the opposite direction. "Say, Amber, there's something I've been meaning to ask you."

"Yes?"

"Remember when the police arrested Edna and Sergeant Smith asked her if she wanted to waive her rights?"

"I remember. I caught her eye and shook my head a little, and then she asked for a lawyer."

"Right. I was just wondering why you did that."

"She looked so old and scared, and I felt sorry for her. The police can be very intimidating."

"That's true," I agreed.

"Why do you ask? Don't tell me you think *I* had something to do with Matt's murder."

"Of course not," I said quickly. "I was just curious; that's all." What I didn't say was that, of all the people in the house at the time of Matt's murder, Amber seemed the least likely suspect.

My answer seemed to satisfy Amber, and as we went our own ways, I thought about all the other people in Matt's house that day. Since I no longer considered Edna a suspect, one of them must be the killer. But which one? My head was jumbled with the various motives they had. I went back to the classic standard for determining who might be a murderer: motives, means, and opportunity. The means couldn't be clearer: Matt had obviously been smothered with Jennifer's blue beaded pillow, and since most of the people in the house that day had had the opportunity to creep into Matt's sickroom while Edna snoozed in the sunroom, the determining factor in finding Matt's killer always came back to motive. Unfortunately, several people had motives, and it was difficult to sort out whose was the strongest.

When I arrived at Jennifer's house, I discovered the entire area jammed with parked cars on both sides of the street, so I circled the block and found a spot on a side street. I hadn't heard from Wes yet, but I'd forgotten to turn my phone back on after the funeral. I waited impatiently for the few seconds it took for my smartphone to show a display. Sure enough: there was a text message from Wes, telling me his flight had landed in Des Moines on time, and he should be back in Center City by late afternoon. I called him back right away, and we confirmed our plans for a romantic dinner later at Arnold's, the restaurant where we'd gone on our first date.

Happy to have our dinner to look forward to, I climbed out of the car and started walking. As I rounded the corner, Justin's red Corvette flew by. I caught a glimpse of Chloe in the passenger seat as the sports car passed. When I arrived at Jennifer's, the red 'vette was parked in the driveway, and Jennifer, her parents, and Justin were getting out of a black limousine while their chauffeur held the door open for them. Obviously, Bunny had been driving Justin's car, and if Chloe hadn't agreed to come today, Bunny would have been driving it back from the funeral alone.

I stood back so that the family could enter the house ahead of me and other people who were arriving. Then we all followed them inside, where Jennifer and her mother turned left and went into the living room, and her father went into the den, offering the guests who had already gathered there drinks from a makeshift bar set up in the corner of the large room. A long table, draped in white linens and laden with food for the guests, had been set up against one wall and the furniture in the room rearranged to accommodate it.

Liz and the colonel had already arrived, and since they were standing near the bar when Jennifer's father arrived, he offered them drinks. While they waited, Liz saw me and motioned for me to join them. Like Liz, I decided on a glass of white wine. The colonel opted for beer, and as soon as we had drinks in hand, we retreated to a quieter corner of the crowded room, and I pressed Liz to tell me all about her trip to Florida. It sounded delightful, especially the warm weather, and I hoped she wouldn't regret coming back earlier than she'd planned, considering the snowstorm forecast for the next day.

The colonel cast a longing glance toward the buffet just as it was about to be replenished. Carefully balancing a large tray, Nancy came in and set in down on the end of the table. Barb followed her, setting another tray beside the first. They stood back, surveyed the table, rearranged a few items, and left the room after greeting the guests.

"That's quite a spread," the colonel said, nodding toward the table, "and there's another one in the dining room."

"It looks as though Katie has plenty of help," I said.

The colonel knit his brows. "Katie—that's the name you mentioned the other day, when we were talking about my old landscaper, Hank. You thought Katie was his wife's name."

"So sad about Hank," Liz said.

"I wonder how he's getting along," the colonel remarked. "He didn't keep in contact after he gave up his landscaping business."

"Oh, my dear, he died," Liz said. "The last time I talked to him he was trying to get his insurance company to pay for a new treatment his doctor recommended, but they refused."

"You don't happen to remember the name of the

company, do you, Liz?" I asked.

"Iowa, um, something that starts with Iowa, I think."

"Iowa Insurance Plans?"

"That sounds right, but I'm not sure."

Excusing myself, I headed for the kitchen. I'd promised Wes that I wouldn't confront anybody, but I rationalized that there was little harm in having a chat with Katie, and since there were plenty of people in the house, I wouldn't be alone, anyway. Had Katie learned that Matt was a partner in Iowa Insurance Plans for the first time in Mrs. Patton's office? Or had she already known and blamed Matt for withholding treatment and, ultimately, her husband's death? Revenge could be a powerful motive.

I peeked into the kitchen. Katie, Nancy, Barb, Fiona, and Bunny were all absorbed in various tasks, so I decided to wait for a more opportune moment to speak with Katie. They didn't notice me as I cut through the kitchen to the crowded dining room and helped myself to a couple of finger sandwiches and a cookie from the inviting buffet.

Feeling guilty that I hadn't spoken to Jennifer yet, I wandered into the living room. For a déjà-vu moment, I relived our Sunday afternoon book club meeting. Except for Marcie and Tracey, everybody was there who had been at our meeting that day—Jennifer, Cynthia, Amber, Amy, and me. On the coffee table in front of Jennifer sat a tray holding a teapot, a cup and saucer, and a glass of ice water. Cynthia and Amy were sipping tea, and Amber had a glass of red wine.

I greeted Jennifer with a gentle hug and perched on the edge of a high-backed chair while I nibbled a sandwich.

"I should probably go greet the guests in the den," Jennifer said, less than enthusiastically, but she didn't get up. Instead, she pressed her palm to her forehead. "I have such a splitting headache. Maybe I should take something for it first."

Cynthia reached for her handbag. "I have some acetaminophen," she offered.

"No, thanks, Cynthia," Jennifer replied. "Just plain old aspirin works best for me. I'll go get some."

"Let me," I said. "You've had a rough day. Is it in the kitchen?"

"No, in my medicine cabinet upstairs, right off the master bedroom, end of the hall on your left at the top of the stairs. A couple tablets should do it. You don't need to bring the bottle."

"I'll be right back." At least, I'd thought I'd be right back when I said it, but there was a bottleneck in the foyer, and it took a while to get through the crowd. I caught snippets of conversation as I tried to squeeze between people.

"So inappropriate."

"I couldn't believe she wore that clingy, low-cut top and those skin-tight yoga pants to a *funeral*."

"I know. Nancy asked her to wear her coat during the service, but she refused until Justin—"

Finally, I reached the staircase to the second floor. From what I'd heard, I knew the women could only have been talking about Bunny. I could easily imagine Nancy's shocked reaction to Bunny's outfit, although I hadn't observed her clothing myself.

Hurrying up the stairs, I turned left at the top. I'd never been upstairs in Jennifer's house before. A long hallway ran the length of the second floor, and since all the doors were closed, I was glad that Jennifer had told me where the master bedroom was.

The large room was beautifully decorated in soothing tones of blue with Jennifer's spot-on sense of design evident in every detail from the crown molding to the Persian area rug next to the king-size bed.

I went through to the master bath and opened the medicine cabinet, which was sparsely populated with a small inhaler, a tin of cough drops, and a half-empty, large bottle of generic aspirin. Quickly, I palmed two tablets and returned the bottle to the medicine cabinet. The crush in the foyer had dissipated by the time I returned.

"Sorry it took so long," I apologized, handing her the aspirin tablets. "There was quite a crowd in the foyer, so it took me a while to get to the stairs."

"Thanks, Laurel," she said, popping them into her mouth and chasing them with ice water.

"Shouldn't you have some milk with those aspirin?" Cynthia suggested. "I bet you haven't had much to eat today, and it could be hard on your stomach."

"Ta-da." Bunny, covered in a white chef's apron, bustled into the room carrying a mug topped with whipped cream. "This is just what the doctor ordered. I made you some hot chocolate, exactly the way you like it, Mom, with loads of sugar and whipped cream."

Amy and I did a double-take when Bunny called Jennifer "Mom," and Cynthia rolled her eyes, but Jennifer seemed grateful as Bunny set the mug on the tray in front of her.

"Thank you, Bunny. That was very thoughtful of you."

Jennifer picked up the mug and began daintily spooning whipped cream into her mouth. Bunny flashed an I-told-you-so look at Cynthia and looked daggers at me before she returned to the kitchen. She probably still blamed me for her last encounter with the police, but if she'd told the truth in the first place, she wouldn't have had to go through another round of questioning and revise her original statement.

"I know Bunny has her faults," Jennifer said, "but Justin's determined to marry her, and I don't want to have a falling-out with my son. I'm trying to get along with her for Justin's sake."

We nodded. It was a difficult situation, one in which none of us had any experience ourselves, so we were loathe to offer Jennifer advice. Cynthia changed the subject by commenting on what nice tributes the speakers gave for Matt, which led to speculation about why Don had spoken in Marcie's place. Jennifer told us that Marcie had called her only a few minutes before the funeral was scheduled to begin, complaining that she'd suddenly become ill and wouldn't be able to speak. She'd told Jennifer that she was afraid she'd picked up the virulent flu bug that had been widespread in Center City for the past month. At least, Marcie had had the decency to let Jennifer know that she wouldn't speak.

Although Amy and I knew the truth, we remained silent on the subject, since we hoped that Marcie would come to her senses and accept Roger's proposal.

As we talked, several neighbors and other friends of Jennifer's drifted into the living room to see Jennifer, but, perhaps sensing that we were a tight group, none of them stayed long. Jennifer finished her hot chocolate just as Bunny appeared with another mug of hot chocolate and three sugar cookies.

"Oh, my," Jennifer exclaimed, "just like Christmas! When I was a kid, my mom always served hot chocolate and sugar cookies on Christmas Eve," she said wistfully, as Bunny removed the empty mug, replacing it with a full one along with the small plate of cookies.

I had a feeling Bunny had heard the story before, and with that knowledge, she'd found a wedge to ingratiate herself with her future mother-in-law.

Bunny hadn't bothered to offer anyone else cookies, and when Jennifer asked her to bring another plate of them for us, it took her a second to mask the fleeting look of displeasure on her face.

Bunny smiled and said sweetly, "Of course, Mother," prompting more eye-rolling from Cynthia.

"How's your headache?" Amy asked, helping herself to a large cookie after Bunny had brought in a plateful of tempting goodies.

"Much better," Jennifer said as she drained her second mug of hot chocolate and stifled a yawn. "Does it seem a little warm in here, or is it because I just had a hot drink?"

"It does, a bit." Amber said.

Amy nodded. "I think so, too."

I'll adjust the thermostat," Jennifer said, but when she stood up, she wobbled, caught herself, and sat back on the sofa. "I feel a little woozy."

"Maybe you should lie down for a while," Cynthia suggested.

"Oh, but I should be here," Jennifer protested.

"Everybody will understand," Amy said. "I promise you."

"Well, all right. Maybe I will. Laurel, would you mind asking Justin to adjust the heat. I think he's still downstairs in the rec room watching his little cousins."

"I'll find him," I promised, as Cynthia and Amber helped Jennifer to her feet and supported her. They walked with her to the staircase as Amy trailed behind, carrying Jennifer's jacket, which she'd shed when she complained about being warm.

Jennifer looked up at the stairs to the second floor. "I don't think I can make it," she said in a weak voice.

"Downstairs bedroom," I urged as Cynthia and Amber held her tightly. "It's this way," I said, running ahead and leading them through the kitchen and down the short hallway to the bedroom where Matt had died. I was thinking about getting Jennifer to the closest bed, rather than dwelling on the fact that Jennifer's husband had been murdered in this very room, but after Cynthia and Amber had settled Jennifer on the bed, I looked around and saw that it looked once more like the beautiful "after" picture Jennifer had submitted when she'd entered the room decorating contest sponsored by the Center City Paint Company, except for the missing peacock pillow, now sitting in an evidence locker at the police department. The hospital bed had been removed along with all Matt's medications. It seemed odd that the police had released the crime scene so quickly, but Matt had been one of the most prominent businessmen in Center City, and I surmised that some pressure may have been brought to bear for the police to act quickly and not inconvenience the family any more than necessary.

"Try to get some rest, Jennifer," Amy said as Jennifer closed her eyes.

"Do you think she's all right?" Amber whispered.

"I think stress is taking its toll. She should feel better after a little nap," Cynthia said quietly. "I think I'll go find Liz. I saw her come in with the colonel, but I haven't talked to her since she returned from Florida."

"And I better see what my cousin Chloe is up to. I know she's here somewhere, and I need to give her a ride home."

"I think I'll stay with her for a few minutes," Amy volunteered, "in case Jennifer needs something."

"Good idea, and I'll go find Justin so he can turn the heat down," I said, suddenly remembering Jennifer's complaint about the temperature. Cynthia and Amber left the room ahead of me, as I lingered for one last look, reflecting that Jennifer must be very tired to agree to sleep in the room where her husband had been smothered.

When I went back to the kitchen, I found Katie alone

standing at the island, deftly slicing a cucumber with a large chef's knife. Now was the perfect time to talk to her, but I couldn't forget that the last time I'd spoken to a suspect at home in his kitchen, I'd ended up in the hospital with a knife wound. Acutely aware of the potentially lethal weapon Katie held, I positioned myself on the opposite side of the island, well out of her reach.

"Katie," I said, "I was sorry to hear about your husband's death. I'd heard he was ill, but I just learned that he died."

"It's been two years since he died. It seems like a long time, but it's really not so long," she said, sighing. "Matt certainly didn't help," she added.

"What do you mean?"

"Matt was one of the owners of Hank's insurance company. It's a terrible company, and they refused to pay for Hank's treatment. Really terrible," she said bitterly.

"When did you find out that Matt was a partner in the insurance company?" I asked.

"Same as you. At the lawyer's office. If Matt wasn't dead already, I'd kill him myself!" she said fiercely, but she wilted and began sobbing when I went around the island and put my arm around her shoulder. Searching for a box of tissues, I spotted one on the kitchen desk and grabbed it. Pulling out a handful, I gave them to Katie, who dabbed at her eyes and blew her nose.

"Sorry," she mumbled as she pulled open the cabinet door under the double sink and disposed of the tissues.

"There's no need to be sorry, Katie. I lost my own husband five years ago. I know what you're going through." I'd followed her to the sink, and I noticed the top of a double boiler sitting in the left side.

Katie saw me look at the pot and told me Bunny had left it there for her to clean up. I could see the remnants of hot chocolate at the bottom of the pot, and suddenly I could see a lot more than that. Katie pulled some liquid hand soap from beneath the sink and reached for the faucet.

"No," I practically shouted. "Don't touch the sink!" She stepped back, looking at me in confusion. "Listen, Katie, this is very important," I said urgently. "Something's wrong! Don't let anyone touch the sink or that pot. Do you understand? Promise me!"

Wide-eyed, she nodded, and I ran to living room. Nancy was the first person I saw.

"What's wrong, Laurel?" she asked.

"Jennifer may be in trouble," I said. "Do you know if there are any doctors or nurses here?"

"I don't know," she said, panic-stricken.

When I yelled for a doctor, I knew I might be making a fool of myself; in fact, I hoped that was the case, but I doubted it. The room went silent for a split second before a forty-something woman wearing a dark green suit stood.

"I'm a doctor. Is there an emergency?"

"Please come with me," I said. I was shocked as I saw Amy emerge from the powder room because I'd assumed she was still with Jennifer. She caught up to me as we went down the hall. I rushed through the kitchen, with Amy, Nancy, and the doctor following along. As we passed Katie in the kitchen, I said, "Remember, don't let anyone near." Since she was already standing in front of the sink with her arms crossed, I knew she'd taken me seriously the first time.

We rushed down the back hall to the guest room where Jennifer lay and found that she wasn't alone. Bunny stood beside her. There was a glass of water and an overturned prescription bottle on the bed stand that hadn't been there a few minutes earlier.

Bunny took in the parade and immediately said, "I

think she took sleeping pills. I just came in here to check on her."

As the doctor and Nancy rushed to Jennifer's side, I said, "You put the sleeping pills in her hot chocolate. You're the one who gave them to her!"

"That's a lie!" Bunny screeched. "I'm not going to listen to this." She started to leave the room. Amy and I tried to block her, but she was as determined as a sneaky quarterback with the goal line in sight, and she managed to get around us.

I whirled and saw the colonel blocking the door.

"May I be of any assistance, ladies?"

"Stop her!" Amy and I cried in unison, and the colonel obliged. Bunny struggled to get away from him, but he had a grip like a vise.

"Non-responsive," the doctor said, more to herself than to Nancy, who was wringing her hands at her daughter's bedside. "Someone call 9-1-1. We need to get her to the hospital right away!"

None of us had our cell phones with us, and the colonel was busy making sure Bunny didn't go anywhere, so I ran past them and called 9-1-1 from the kitchen phone while a shocked Katie listened to me explaining the emergency.

By this time, a concerned group had gathered in the kitchen. I asked a couple of the men to help the colonel and pointed toward the hallway. When I told the rest of the crowd that Jennifer would be going to the hospital and explained that we needed to clear a path, they all cooperated in vacating the kitchen and the foyer.

I turned to Katie and thanked her for guarding the sink. "Please stay here, Katie. We can't let anybody touch that pot!"

"Don't worry. I won't move," she said with a determined look on her face.

Earlier I'd left my handbag in the living room. I

went to find it so I could call Wes and tell him what had happened, hoping he was back in Center City by now.

"Sweetheart, you caught me. I was going to surprise you and come over early. I'm only a couple blocks from your house right now," he said when I reached him. "You are back from the funeral by now, aren't you?"

"Oh, thank goodness," I said, explaining the situation and giving him the address.

"I'll be right there," he said.

When I went back to look for the colonel and Bunny, he had her confined in the sunroom, and the men I'd asked to help earlier were blocking the door. Seeing the doctor's grave expression on her face when I peeped in the guest room, I felt sick. I hoped we were in time.

Feeling discouraged, I went to the front door to wait for Wes. I could hear the sirens well before the fire department rescue unit and a police car pulled up to the curb, and I was glad to see that Wes was right behind them. The officers recognized him, and they spoke briefly before following the rescue squad into the house.

"Is Bunny secure?" Wes asked me.

"Yes. She's in the sunroom. The colonel's not going to let her go anywhere."

"Any evidence in the guest room?"

"Yes. The water glass and the pill bottle. And there's the chocolate pot in the kitchen sink. Jennifer's mug might still be in the living room, too. I'm not sure."

"Okay. Wait here." Wes beckoned the officers, dispatching one to move everybody out of the living room while the other one followed him. I was standing in the arched doorway to the den when Chloe sidled up to me.

"What's going on?" she asked.

"I'm afraid your friend Bunny is about to be arrested."

"Some friend. When we got here, she ditched me, and I ended up babysitting a bunch of kids with Justin. She's been acting weird all day. First she can't cope without me right beside her, and then she can't stand to have me around. And that's not all. We had to look at Matt in his coffin after the funeral, and Bunny leaned in, real close. Afterwards, she said how good he looked without all those little pock marks on his face. What did she mean by that, anyway?"

"I think she meant that's how he looked right after she smothered him."

I guess I was talking more loudly than I realized because the whole room behind me seemed to take a collective breath before bursting out in chatter.

We stood, peering into the foyer, as the rescue team wheeled Jennifer out. Although she had a breathing apparatus strapped on her face, I could see that her eyes were closed and she wasn't moving. I knew Nancy, her husband, and Barb would go to the hospital immediately.

"You mentioned helping Justin with the kids earlier," I said to Chloe. "Do you know where he is now? We need to find him so he can be with his mother."

Chapter 20

Justin's relatives found him making a snowman with his younger cousins in a nearby park. I could only imagine his shocked reaction when he learned that his mother had been rushed to the hospital and his girlfriend was responsible for her condition. Enough people had overheard me tell Chloe that Bunny had smothered Matt that, within a few minutes, all the guests at Jennifer's house knew about the allegation.

In the controlled chaos that followed as the house hosted a second major crime scene within a week, Wes took charge while he waited for Lieutenant Walker to arrive. Wes had notified him of the circumstances as soon as I called him, but Walker didn't show up right away, and I could tell Wes was growing impatient. We were standing in the foyer, and I was repeating all the details I knew when the lieutenant and Sergeant Smith finally arrived, in no apparent hurry.

Wes went outside to meet them, and they spoke for several minutes. I heard raised voices a few times, and I distinctly heard Wes say, "It's *your* collar" before all three came into the house.

Wes leaned over and said quietly, "They want to interview you at the station. I'm going with you. Let me drive, and we'll pick your car up later."

I nodded, grateful that he would be accompanying me to the interview. It would be an awkward situation for all of us if Smith interviewed me. For the second time that week, I had to call on my neighbors Fran and Brian to take care of Bear. They often dined out in the evening, so I felt lucky that they'd planned a binge movie night with pizza at home.

As we drove through Center City, I worried about Jennifer, and I asked Wes to call the hospital to find out if there was any news about her condition. I figured the hospital wouldn't tell me anything if I called to check on Jennifer, but they would release information to a police officer. He agreed to call, even though the attempted murder wasn't his case. I had a feeling he might be taking more flack from Walker later for interfering, but he didn't hesitate.

"No word yet," he told me after his first call. Later, while we waited in his office for Walker or Smith to return to the station to interview me, Wes called the hospital again and reported, "touch and go." When Wes told me that, I started crying. I felt sick, knowing that Jennifer might die. Wes wrapped his arms around me and assured me I'd done everything I could, but I still felt anxious.

It wasn't until several hours later, during my interview with Smith, that we finally learned that Jennifer was on the mend and expected to make a full recovery.

I'd really hoped Walker would conduct my interview, rather than Smith. Wes insisted on sitting in, and Smith offered no objection when he sat beside me, rather than her. We were all excessively polite to each other as the interview proceeded. When Smith asked me how I figured out that Bunny had given Jennifer sleeping pills, I told her about seeing the chocolate pot in the sink, Bunny's serving Jennifer hot chocolate but not offering it to any of the guests, and Jennifer's sleepy reaction after she'd had two mugs of hot chocolate. Then I launched into my reasons for believing that Bunny had not only tried to murder Jennifer but had also killed Matt.

"Bunny had a strong motive—money, and that's what really convinced me that she was trying to do away with Jennifer and that she'd smothered Matt. She made a mistake when she thought killing Matt would make Justin rich, though, because Matt had changed his will without Justin's knowledge. That's why she was so outraged when she found out that Jennifer would inherit most of Matt's estate, instead of Justin, and that's why she urged Justin to contest the will.

"He didn't want to contest it, though, but I know for a fact that she kept badgering him about it. I guess she must have finally realized that he wasn't going to go along with her. With Jennifer out of the way, Justin stood to inherit everything, and Bunny was counting on Justin's promise to marry her. She could have settled for the million dollars that Matt left her if she agreed not to marry Justin, but she was too greedy for that; she wanted it all. She'd already killed once to get her hands on the money, so it wasn't too much of a leap for her to target Jennifer. I think she planned to stage Jennifer's death as an accidental overdose."

Smith listened without commenting, and after I'd told her about every detail I could think of, she said she'd have my formal statement prepared, and I could either wait to sign it or come in to do it the next day.

"I'll wait," I said. "I'd just as soon get this over with."

"We'll be in my office," Wes told Smith as she left the interview room.

Wes turned to me and grumbled, "Some homecoming."

"Maybe this will make it better," I said, putting my arms around him and pulling him close for a long kiss.

"Better," he agreed.

* * *

Charged with first-degree murder and attempted

murder, Bunny refused to admit what she'd done in the days that followed. She couldn't afford an attorney, and, unbelievably, she had the temerity to ask Justin if he'd pay for a lawyer to defend her, but he'd finally recognized Bunny for who she was, and he wanted nothing more to do with her. She had to settle for a public defender.

Although there was plenty of physical evidence against Bunny connecting her to the attempt on Jennifer's life, there was none linking her to Matt's death. The district attorney's case against Bunny was circumstantial, but it definitely met the motive-means-and-opportunity test. The last I heard, Bunny's lawyer was trying to negotiate a plea deal.

Edna was released the day after Bunny doctored Jennifer's hot chocolate. I later learned that Bunny had also mixed some other medication into the frosting that she'd put on the sugar cookies she served Jennifer. I was sure Bunny had slipped some of the beads from the pillow she used to smother Matt into Edna's pocket to implicate her, but there was no way to prove it.

True to form, Edna didn't thank me for figuring out who the real killer was. When I ran into her at the community center a few days after her release from the county detention center, she asked, "What took you so long?" and complained that it was *my* fault that she'd been locked up for over a week.

As for FFF, our board voted to take the evidence of Marcie's embezzlement to the police because we never saw her or heard from her again. With a push from Jennifer, Mrs. Patton agreed to release Matt's bequest to FFF, despite there being little likelihood that we'd ever see a penny of the embezzled money returned.

FFF faces an uphill battle to regain the trust of its donors, but our temporary director is already making some inroads. After learning that a popular councilwoman who supported downtown parking development planned to run for mayor, Cynthia decided not to throw her hat into the ring, and I suggested to our board that she'd make a perfect interim director for FFF. I kept my promise to Josh, too, advocating and winning a salary increase for FFF's underpaid staff.

After one of our board meetings, I saw Chloe in the FFF office and couldn't resist satisfying my curiosity about the topic of conversation between her and Matt the day Amy saw them talking outside the office. Saying she knew nothing about FFF's financial business, Chloe denied tipping Matt off about the embezzlement, but I did find out what they were talking about. Matt had asked Chloe out on a date, but she'd turned him down. As she put it, "I don't date married men, and, besides, he was old enough to be my grandfather. Eww!"

Jennifer and I had lunch the other day, and I was surprised to see that she'd gained weight, and the tiny wrinkles Matt had complained about on her face had all but disappeared, thanks to the additional pounds. Understandably, she still harbored mixed feelings about Matt. I doubted that they'd ever be resolved because he had been so much a part of her life for over twenty years.

Although she felt at loose ends, she was considering starting a home decorating business. Many women who possessed her wealth would have opted to lead the life of the idle rich, but Jennifer wanted to make her own job using her design skills to launch a business. I didn't know anything about her business acumen, but I did know she was a superb designer, and I wished her all the best with her new endeavor. She could certainly afford to hire a business manager, anyway, so that she could concentrate on the creative side of the business.

I was glad that life in Hawkeye Haven was returning

to normal, and I was even happier when spring arrived, and we enjoyed the first warm day in months. It also happened to be the day of Amy's big dance competition. Cynthia, Pete, Wes, and I, along with Bud's new girlfriend Sandy, all attended the finals to cheer on Amy and Bud. They won second place for their foxtrot, but they did even better in their Latin dances, taking first prize in both tango and cha-cha. We insisted on taking the proud duo to dinner to celebrate their triumph, and it was after midnight when Wes took me home.

Bear heard us coming and started barking before we opened the front door. He stopped making a racket as soon as I petted him, but he refused to settle down until I'd given him a treat and Wes had indulged him with a tummy rub.

"Would you like something to drink?" I asked Wes, after Bear flopped down on his bed in the den. I knew he'd be asleep in minutes.

"Sure. The usual," he said.

After I poured him a beer and myself a glass of white wine, we sat on the sofa in the den while I chattered about the dance competition. It took me a while to notice that Wes wasn't saying very much. In fact, he was looking at me with an odd expression on his face.

"What is it, Wes?" I asked.

"Oh, uh, um, I was just thinking." He hesitated. Wes wasn't normally tongue-tied, so my radar kicked in.

"Yes?"

"Um, I was thinking—wouldn't a Mississippi River steamboat make a great place for our honeymoon?"

Recipes and DIY Diva Pillow Projects

Katie's Dressed-Up Granny Apple Salad

Katie serves this salad to Jennifer's guests any time of the year. It's easy to increase or decrease the ingredients to suit individual tastes.

Ingredients

8 cups mixed salad greens (an 11- or 12-ounce package can be used if you're in a hurry)

2 Granny Smith apples, diced

1/4 cup dried cranberries

1/4 cup chopped walnuts

1/2 cup bleu cheese crumbles

1/2 cup sweet Vidalia onion dressing

Rinse, tear, and dry salad greens. Dice two Granny Smith apples, but do not peel the apples before dicing. Leave the peel on each apple for added crunch and a pretty green color. Add the diced apples and salad dressing to the mixed greens and toss until the greens are well coated. Sprinkle cranberries, walnuts, and bleu cheese crumbles on the top and serve.

Makes six to eight servings

Amy's Corn Casserole

This is a hearty dish, and Amy especially likes to serve it at Thanksgiving, Christmas, or Easter.

Ingredients

2 14.75-ounce cans creamed corn

1 small yellow onion

1 small green pepper

1 sleeve saltine crackers (salted)

coarse black pepper

Dice onion and green pepper. Pulverize one package stack of saltine crackers. Amy puts them in a large, sealed plastic bag and pounds them with a rolling pin before finishing by rolling the rolling pin over the bag several times. Of course, it might be easier to make the crumbs by using a food processor! Combine corn, onion, green pepper, and cracker crumbs in a mixing bowl, and transfer the mixture to a 1 1/2-quart baking dish. Sprinkle pepper over the top and bake at 325 degrees for an hour.

Makes six servings

Amber's Ginger Cookies

Amber loves to make desserts, and cookies are her specialty.

3/4 cup butter
1 cup sugar
1 egg
5 tablespoons molasses
2 cups flour
2 teaspoons baking soda
2 teaspoons ginger
2 teaspoons cinnamon
1/2 teaspoon salt
Extra granulated sugar for coating

Soften butter at room temperature so that it's easy to mix. Cream butter and sugar. Add the egg and beat well. Sift dry ingredients and add to the mixture. Mix well. Roll the dough in balls, about 1 1/2 inch in diameter. Keep the size of the balls consistent. Roll each ball in granulated sugar. Set balls evenly on ungreased cookie sheet. Bake at 350 degrees for 10 minutes.

Makes about three dozen cookies.

Tracey's Iowa Pork Tenderloin Sandwich

As a Seattle native, Tracey had never heard of a pork tenderloin sandwich before she moved to Iowa. She discovered that restaurants all over the state serve their version of the sandwich, which features a six- to eight-inch-diameter flattened, breaded, and fried pork tenderloin on a regular size hamburger bun. Of course, if you prefer, it can be dressed up with a larger fancy bun and all sorts of veggies and condiments. Tracey prefers only dill pickles and ketchup on hers.

Ingredients

1 pork tenderloin (about 1 pound)

½ cup whole milk

2 eggs

½ cup flour

1 cup Panko bread crumbs

1 sleeve saltine crackers

½ teaspoon salt

½ teaspoon pepper

peanut oil

4 hamburger buns

1. Cut pork tenderloin into four equal pieces. Cut about three-quarters through each piece and spread to butterfly it. Put in a large sandwich bag or cover with plastic wrap and pound with a meat mallet until about ¼-inch thick.

2. In a mixing bowl, beat eggs, add milk, and beat well. Set aside.

3. Pulverize the crackers in a food processor or by putting them in a one gallon baggie and pounding them with a mallet.

4. In a flat pan mix flour, bread crumbs, cracker crumbs, salt, and pepper.

5. Dredge tenderloins, one at a time, in egg mixture, and then in the crumb mixture, coating well on both sides so that the coating is as thick as possible without dropping off.

6. Pour about ¾ inch to one inch of peanut oil into an iron skillet, large enough to accommodate each breaded tenderloin piece.

7. Heat oil to 350 degrees over medium heat. When the oil is hot enough, pan fry each breaded tenderloin piece, one at a time, about 2 to 3 minutes per side, until golden brown.

8. When done, remove from oil, and drain on paper towels.

9. Serve on a bun with condiments of your choice.

Makes four sandwiches.

Bud's Fringed Leather Pillow

Bud isn't exactly a whiz at sewing, so he devised a way to make a pillow without sewing a stitch.

Materials Needed

leather or suede, either genuine or synthetic

13 yards 1/8-inch-width leather or suede lacing (for 18-inch square pillow)

square pillow form

scratch awl

Instructions

You will need two square pieces of leather, one inch larger than your pillow form. For example, if you're making an eighteen-inch square pillow, you will need two nineteen-inch pieces of leather. It's a good idea to make a pattern for your square before you shop for material, whether it's a real leather hide, an old coat from the thrift store, or synthetic material from the fabric store. Place your pattern on the leather to determine whether there's enough for your project, and remember that you will need to cut two squares of leather.

Instructions

1. Place the pattern on the material, tape it to the wrong side of the leather, and cut out with sharp scissors. Regular scissors should work fine. You don't need to use your good fabric

scissors on leather. Cut two squares.

2. Place wrong sides together (they will go on the inside of the pillow). Optional: You can hold these in place with plastic chip clips if you wish, but be careful not to mar the leather.

3. For the fringe, you will need approximately 12 2/3 yards of one-eighth-inch-wide leather or suede. You can hand cut these from the same leather used for the pillow, or you can purchase leather or suede lacing that is already cut to the correct width.

4. With the scratch awl, mark and make a hole through both layers about 1/4 inch from the edge of the leather. Be careful not to make the hole too close to the edge.

5. Cut a six-inch length of leather lacing, angling the ends, double it, and poke the doubled end through both holes. You may need to use a tiny crochet hook or a blunt needle to coax it through. Pull it up to form a small loop and thread both ends through the loop and tighten.

6. Repeat at one-inch intervals. When you get to the fourth side, insert the pillow form before finishing the fringe on the last side.

Lacy Neck Roll Pillow

Laurel introduced this lacy neck roll pillow to her class. It makes a perfect accent if you want to add a feminine touch to bedroom decor. There are several ways to vary its look. Use the same color lace, satin, and ribbon, or use contrasting or coordinating colors to make the pattern on the lace stand out. You can add ribbon, bow, and rosette decorations, if you like. Since this is a sewing project, you'll need a sewing machine, fabric scissors, tape measure, straight edge, marking tools, pins, and thread to match your lace and satin.

Materials Needed

1 6"x14" neck roll pillow form

2/3 yard 36"-width galloon (both edges scalloped) Chantilly lace

2/3 yards (any width) lightweight satin or charmeuse fabric

1 yard 1/4" double-faced satin ribbon

Note: galloon lace in a 36" width may be difficult to find, or it may be very expensive. If you're not able to find this lace, you can use lace that is scalloped on just one edge. In this case, you will need 1 1/3 yards, so that you can make your own double-edged lace by sewing two pieces together with a seam in the middle that you can cover with a wide single-faced satin ribbon.

Instructions

    1.   Measure around the center of your neck roll pillow form, add one inch to the measurement, and cut your lace to that width.

    2.   Cut a rectangle of satin 34" long with a width the same as you used to cut the width of your lace.

    3.   With wrong sides together, sew a 1/2" seam the length of the satin.

    4.   Make a narrow hem on both raw edges of the satin.

    5.   Press seams and turn so that right side is facing out. Pull the satin casing over the pillow form so that there is an equal amount of satin on each side of the form.

    6.   On one side, gather the excess satin in the center and tie a sturdy thread around it. Secure the thread with a square knot and clip close to the knot, taking care not to cut it. Repeat for the other side.

    7.   With wrong sides together, sew a 1/2"

seam the length of the lace.

8.   Press seams and turn so that right side is facing out. Pull the lace casing over the satin-covered pillow form and center it.

9.   Gather lace on each side and tie 1/2 yard of ribbon around each end over the tied thread. Secure the ribbon with a knot and tie in a bow. Adjust the bows and cut the ribbon ends on the diagonal.

ABOUT THE AUTHOR

An instructor at five colleges over the years, Paula Darnell most often taught the dreaded first-year English composition classes, but she's also been happy to teach some fun classes, such as fashion design, sewing, and jewelry making. Paula has a Bachelor's degree in English from the University of Iowa, Iowa City, and a Master's degree in English from the University of Nevada, Reno.

Like Laurel, the main character in Paula's DIY Diva Mystery series, Paula enjoys all kinds of arts and crafts. Some of her memorable projects include making a hat and a cape to wear to Royal Ascot, sewing wedding gowns for both her daughters, exhibiting her textile and mixed-media artwork in juried art shows, and having one of her jewelry projects accepted for inclusion in *Leather Jewelry,* published by Lark Books. She sells some of her jewelry and hair accessories in her Etsy shop: www.etsy.com/shop/PaulaDJewelry.

Paula's interest in DIY craft projects and fashion led to her writing hundreds of articles for print and online national publications. She is the author of *Death by Association* and *Death by Design*, both in her cozy series, the DIY Diva Mysteries. You can visit her author website at https://www.pauladarnellauthor.com/ to read about upcoming books and subscribe to her Cozy Mystery Newsletter.

Paula lives in Las Vegas, Nevada, with her husband Gary and their 110-pound dog Rocky, whose favorite pastime is lurking in the kitchen, hoping for a handout

www.ingramcontent.com/pod-product-compliance
Lightning Source LLC
Chambersburg PA
CBHW020318260626
47156CB00004B/1269